YOU'LL LIKE MY MOTHER

Naomi A. Hintze

YOU'LL LIKE MY MOTHER

G. P. PUTNAM'S SONS
NEW YORK

For HSH

YOU'LL LIKE MY MOTHER

Chapter 1

I CAN REMEMBER biting my nails on the bus that afternoon, a habit I thought I had broken. I remember thinking about the way the map looked when I was trying to get up the courage to make this trip. I had bought the biggest map I could find and, crying, spread it out on that rickety little table in that terrible little room in Los Angeles.

The Ohio River had been a crooked blue line, followed faithfully by the red line of Route 52 until the place where, about two inches east of Cincinnati, the river made a jog southward. On that southward jog I had seen for the first time on any map the town that was Always, Ohio. The town whose existence I had almost come to doubt.

The letters I had sent there had never had an answer.

Until this Tuesday afternoon, my trip had been as unreal as the lines and dots on the map. But the single black line that the map showed spurring south from the main highway had now become a jolting reality of potholed macadam.

Air conditioning on the plane that had brought me to Cincinnati, on the bus that had brought me to the Ar-Kay Motel back there on 52, had cooled the air to a bearable, if flavorless, 72 degrees. But the open windows of this lum-

9

bering local let in the oppressive humidity of a June with too much rain; the reek of steaming barnyards; the cloying, ether type of sweetness of red clover.

Until today, all those who had helped me eastward were a faceless blur, because I hadn't looked at one of them. This bus driver with the very dark red hair I would always remember. He was young, and he wore Army fatigues. Brown-eyed, he watched me in the rearview mirror. A few other passengers, some three or four, had gotten off at houses along the way, and now I was the only one left on the bus to Always.

In my twenty-one years I have had—forgive me—my share of glances, passes, what-have-you. But let me clue you in: I wore a tent dress, almost the same tan as my short hair; it was made of that marvelous material you can wash and wear in an hour unless the humidity is up around 100, the way it seemed to be today.

I had been washing and wearing this marvelous little tent almost every day for about four months now. In a little less than three weeks—if my doctor back in Los Angeles knew how to read that clever little thing he had consulted —I would be able to throw it away.

I was so pregnant I had forgotten all about how to be a girl, and although I supposed the time might come when I'd want to remember again, that time certainly was not now.

I had to keep changing my position so the baby would not kick so crossly. My feet had swollen a little; I wore canvas, rubber-soled sandals which I had bought yesterday in the rain in Cincinnati, a size larger than I usually wear. They were cheap, with ugly stripes (normally I am an awful shoe snob), but they, with this dress, would soon be thrown away. Or given if I could find somebody grindingly poor and with no taste whatever.

The driver said, "Why don't you move up front where you'll be more comfortable?"

He meant, *Let's talk.*

"I'm fine here." I put my head back and tried to look comfortable. *As the airline stewardess said when she quit her job, "I've got straight teeth and a friendly manner, only I'm sick of smiling."*

"Nice people run that motel back there on 52 where I picked you up."

"Yes." I had spent last night there, but I hadn't looked at anyone. I didn't want to talk to anyone now in this half hour or so before we would get to Always. I needed to worry. I needed to rehearse the lines I would say and maybe change some of them.

"The Ar-Kay Motel. His name's Arthur, and her name's Kay."

Clever. Beautiful. I didn't say anything, just closed my eyes, pretending I thought I could sleep.

Matthew's voice: *You look so vulnerable when you are asleep. You look like the sort of girl somebody must always take care of. Francesca, Francesca.* I never had liked my name until I heard Matthew say it. He used to whisper it over and over. The tires of the bus whispered it now. *Francesca, Francesca . . .*

I opened my eyes and sat up straighter and looked out at the bright, hot countryside with its distant glimpses of brimming river. The time was past for letting myself think about Math all the time, for the sick indulgence of letting myself listen to him whispering my name.

Maybe I ought to move up front, I thought. That nice young driver looked like Albert Finney in *Tom Jones.* (I had sat through so many movies in the past several months that now everybody looked like somebody I had seen in some movie.) The driver would ask a question or

11

two, and I would say, *I am on my way east to see my father.* No, leave out my father. *I am on my way east and am stopping by Always to call on my mother-in-law. You may know her. The name is Kinsolving. Mrs. Matthew Kinsolving, Senior.*

It would not be necessary to tell him that I had never met her, had never had any answers to my letters to her. But it was quite possible that he would volunteer some information that would satisfactorily explain.

No. There could not be a satisfactory explanation. I stopped biting my nails, reminding myself that I had moved to a new plateau where I was not allowing myself to be swamped again by last fall's feelings of total rejection, total despair.

When I first got the news last September telling of Matthew's death en route to Vietnam, I had sent her a telegram, not knowing whether or not she would have been informed by military sources. I was all alone in L.A., but there had been many words of sympathy and explanation from those whose job it is to take care of such matters. On tape, they told me, somebody had caught the pilot's last half-dozen words and these last sounds that meant forever over and out. *Don't hope,* they said to me. *You cannot get over this until you accept it.*

I had sent another telegram to tell Matthew's mother when the service would be, that bleak and empty service they have when there is nothing to send back. No dust; no dog tags; not even the gold wedding band that matched my own. There had been a man in uniform to stand beside me when they put the folded flag in my hands.

My first letter to my mother-in-law had been very long, full of grief and love. I knew that the rules of etiquette said she should have written to me when she first heard Matthew was marrying me, welcoming me into the family, but I threw all formality aside and told her how it had been for Matthew and me from the beginning.

I told her how, in July, he had found me there in that shack on the beach, not far from death with blood poisoning. How he had saved my life. How, late in August, he had married me, although I knew he had written her. "We wanted to do things properly, come to see you. But we had so little time. . . ."

There had been no answer. Nor had there been any answer to the shorter, more restrained letter I sent in November when I wrote her that I was having Matthew's child.

Both telegrams had been delivered—by messenger since there was no telephone; I had checked on that. The letters, too, must have been delivered. I had talked to the mailman one day, and he told me that if she had died or moved away, the letters would have been returned to me, rubber-stamped with an appropriate checking of the reason for failure to deliver.

I sat on my hands so I would not bite my nails anymore and stared along the road that was taking me to Always. *No, she is not dead. She is alive and living there in that big house on the river that Math told me about. And she hates me.*

There were many mothers, I knew, who automatically hated the girls their sons married, under whatever circumstances. It seemed to be one of those cliché situations of which life is so full. Matthew was an only child, and his relationship with his mother had been a very close one. Add to that the fact that he had not gone back to spend his last leave with her before going to Vietnam but instead had married a girl he had known for a very short time. Wasn't that, for a certain type of mother, enough?

Yes, it was enough, and I was not going to torture myself

13

with any further wondering. I would not wonder if there might have been some way for Mrs. Kinsolving to find out why I was in that beach shack where her son found me, half dying, too far gone to care when a stranger walked in and saw me there in that faded bikini I hadn't had off in five days. I would not let myself wonder if she might have found out about what happened at Merriam College. A thousand times I had said to myself, *It's a small world. Merriam College is well known. Girls from all over the country go there. What if—*

Here on this bus today it was too late to wonder.

I twisted, changing my position. My back was hurting a little the way it did sometimes these days now that the baby was so heavy. I let my eyes slide past the watching eyes in the mirror up front and turned to dig in my big straw bag for a compact and lipstick. I wiped powder from the little mirror and looked into a face that didn't look like anybody's face, not even mine. Blue eyes were smudged with shadow, although I had not put it there. I jabbed a little color against my mouth, moving my lips together as if I cared about having them glisten.

Matthew had told me I should forgive myself, put all that had happened behind me. *All right, Math, I am trying. I want to like myself again. I want to do what is right for my peace of mind and for the baby. That's why I am on this bus that's taking me to Always. Scared to pieces. You know me.*

Yesterday at the Agency in Cincinnati the woman sitting behind a big, glass-topped desk had listened very carefully to my reasons for giving up the baby for adoption. Her name was Miss Gee. She had small, real-looking pearls in her ears.

I had felt calm when I first started talking to her. "For the baby's sake, I am trying to be very realistic about all this, to recognize my limits. I have had a lot of time to think in these last few months, and I believe I have begun to know myself."

"It is good to know yourself."

"I know, for instance, that I have never been a fighter. It would take a fighter, it seems to me, to bring up a child on the small allotment I will have from the government. I would have to leave the baby in a day nursery and get a job. I wouldn't be able to get much of a job because I quit college before I was prepared to do anything that would pay me a decent salary."

Miss Gee murmured, her eyes on my face, that it would probably be difficult.

"It's not that I would mind working hard, but I feel very strongly that a child needs two parents. My own mother died when I was born. My father remarried when I was eleven, and . . . well, pretty soon they had their own family. I know from experience that a child needs two parents who love him." I had steadied my hands, suddenly trembling, on the glass-topped desk.

Miss Gee nodded and said carefully, "That, of course, is the ideal situation."

"But I know I have a tendency to look back on mistakes. I don't want to make any more big mistakes that I'll have to blame myself for. That's why I feel that before I decide definitely to give up this child for adoption, I must go to see my mother-in-law."

A flicker in her eyes made me think that until that moment she had not thought I was married.

"I understand that after a girl has given up her baby and a certain amount of time has gone by, there's not anything she can do about it."

"That's usually true."

"Well, there is a chance—" I forced a small laugh, "like

one in a million—that my mother-in-law might want the baby. Or might need us both, or something." I broke it off, not wanting my voice to betray me. I was sure Miss Gee had more than her share of self-pitying girls in this office.

"You should go to see her, of course. She knows you are coming?"

"No. She . . . it seems she doesn't have a phone right now. I tried to look it up this morning before I came to see you, and her name wasn't listed. But I am sure she still lives there."

"I see," she said, but not as if she did. She made a great show of straightening the few papers into a neat pile, as if it had to be done precisely before she looked up. "Everything may very well work out just beautifully. But if it should not, do you have a place where you can go?"

Could I say no?

"Oh, yes. I can go to my father in Massachusetts." I smiled at her brightly, seeing myself going up the steps of that little red Cape Cod where Father lived with Allegra and their four children. It was the smallest house in the best section of the most exclusive Boston suburb. On my knees, that is.

Allegra. She had spit on her teeth when she laughed. That was the first thing I noticed about her when she first came into my life, that and the archly naughty way she would roll her eyes at my father and make with the double meanings so beloved by that generation and so sickening to me when I had known the terse Anglo-Saxon for everything for years. Allegra, now, with her four pale, perfect children, who won DAR medals which she wore on a chain around her fat wrist.

My father. The study of that little Cape Cod was crammed with genealogical records and copies of kings' grants and notes for his book about the Cabbot family with two *b*'s. *Never,* said my father, *forget who you are.*

I had forgotten. It was not in him to forgive me for what I had done.

Miss Gee had her papers all straight, and she had opened and closed each drawer at least twice. She came out from behind her desk and held out her hand. "Good luck, my dear. Go to see your mother-in-law. I shall be thinking about you and hoping that things work out happily for everyone concerned."

"Thank you. You might keep your fingers crossed."

She laughed and held up crossed fingers. "We'll be glad to help in any way we can. If you should decide in favor of adoption, you can come back and fill out the forms and all that. But I have a feeling that, one way or another, you're going to be able to keep that baby."

But I didn't want to keep it. To myself now with a feeling of bleak inadequacy I could admit it. I didn't think I was the type to be a good mother. I remembered Allegra, all toothy ecstasy over each advent, but I couldn't seem to make myself feel any of that. At first it had bothered me, but my doctor hadn't been the sort with whom I could discuss emotional hang-ups. A bored, George Sanders type, he always got the business of examination over quickly and then turned me over to his nurse.

On my first visit to the office she had given me a little booklet that showed me a picture of the bean that was growing inside me. It was shaped like a bean, curved over, thumb to nose, mostly head, and great places for eyes. A fetus. I had found it easy enough to resist loving something called a fetus.

Of course I knew that the baby looked different now that it was almost ready to be born. My date was for late in June if my reckoning was right. The baby could come

17

two weeks early or two weeks late, my doctor had said. Lately I had noticed a tightening, a periodic drawing up of abdominal muscles, that I assumed was a practicing for the great effort needed for birth. But the bright, chatty little book never explained that nor told me much of anything else that was helpful.

Under Chapter Nine (the numeral drawn ever so humorously to represent a bulging female who could not see her feet) it said, "And now you, the producer, are almost ready! There is a hum of activity in the wings! The audience (your husband) is beginning to get restless. And the star, your baby. . . ."

I was glad the book was written that way. It was easy to reject such whimsy. The physical act of birth, I supposed, might result in some emotional change. And I knew that if I were ever to hold it in my arms, see Matthew's eyes. . . .

But I did not intend to hold it in my arms. I did not intend to see it at all.

The brakes were applied suddenly. I grabbed the seat ahead of me to brace myself, and we hit a hole in the road. The driver was the one who groaned. "I'm sorry. Only, look—*please*. You're sitting right over the back wheels. And the shock absorbers on this old crate. . . ."

"I know." I met the brown eyes in the mirror. "Maybe I should move—"

"Wait. Don't try to get up until I stop." He slowed and moved the bus to the side of the road, then busied himself with lighting a cigarette.

All willowy grace, I made my way forward and edged into the seat just behind him.

He turned, offered me a cigarette.

"No, thanks." I saw the way he looked at the ring on my left hand, and I thought: *What is there about me that makes people wonder if I am an unmarried mother? Is there a dissolute look? An unprotected, unloved, no-husband look?*

He drew on his cigarette and gave me a glance. "I bet if your husband knew what a rattletrap this bus is and how rough the road is, he'd pitch a fit."

I let my mind slide past this obvious probe for information into a moment of pretense that was warm and good. Oh, how blessed if I had to answer to Matthew tonight for this foolish risk to my precious self and our precious child. For this one moment, to this bus driver, my husband was alive.

There had been such a moment back in November in L.A. An acquaintance who did not know of Matthew's death leaned from a passing car to call, "How's Math?" I had waved. "Fine." And for a few seconds felt good about it, comforted by the thought that in one mind Matthew Kinsolving still lived.

But I was through with that sort of pretending, just as I was through with hoping I would dream about him each night. I said, "My husband is dead. He was killed on his way to Vietnam." And then, very fast to save him embarrassment and forestall any words of pity he might feel necessary, I added, "He lived at Always. His mother still lives there. Kinsolving. . . ."

"Kinsolving. . . . I know that name. They have a big house on the point out in the river."

"Right." Matthew had told me.

"They used to be rich. Used to own a mill. There was a son away at school all the time. My age, or a couple of years younger."

"He was twenty-three."

He eased the bus into gear and raised his voice to say, "Well, I never knew him, and I never knew the family. My home is at that little town back up there on the highway where the motel is. I've been away. The Army; med school next fall. My Uncle Leo owns this bus—I just drive it on vacation for the hell of it. And because I'm broke."

It seemed polite to smile a little. "So you're going to be a doctor." Not that I cared.

"If I'm not, don't tell my mother. You know, 'my son, the—'" His eyes met mine, so much closer now in the mirror. He grinned. "She's got one who's a lawyer. One who's a priest. Seven of us. She names it, and we do it."

A thought came rather drearily: If I should marry again —years from now—what total revenge to marry somebody like this, probably, hopefully, with a name like Rafferty or O'Shaughnessy. O my father, you with your rubbings from ancient English gravestones to prove that Cabbot is properly spelled with two *b*'s!

But resentment was destructive, and revenge was beneath me. Matthew, who thought more highly of me than I did of myself, told me that once. He had been so good for me, so steadying. I might have turned into a fairly decent human being with him here to help me. Even my father would have approved of Matthew Kinsolving. And —who knows?—might very well have turned into the sort of parent who would say to a child, *Remember who you are.*

I brought my mind back to what the red-haired driver was telling me. He was talking about his Uncle Leo who, it seemed, knew everything there was to know about everybody in this part of Ohio.

"He makes everybody's business his business. Whenever he sees newspapers piled up on somebody's porch, say, he stops to find out why. If Uncle Leo had been driving this bus today and you had asked him one question about the Kinsolving family, he wouldn't have stopped talking till he had told you the name of everybody in the family and the grades they made in school clear back to the Civil War."

I wished his Uncle Leo had been driving this bus today. He might have been able to give me the one illuminating bit of truth that would have allowed me to stay, in all conscience, right on this bus until it made the round trip back to my motel on 52. In Cincinnati then, tomorrow, I could have gone back to the agency and filled out those forms and let Miss Gee make all the arrangements.

There was an increasing straggle of houses now on either side of the road. I clutched my straw bag tight, knowing a sudden lurch of dread. Something flashed through my mind that I had not thought of in years. Back in Bewdley Hall, the boarding school my father and Allegra had sent me to when they got married, there was a mean girl who called me Francesca, the Gutless Wonder. I had laughed loudly with the other girls about it and then cried alone later, knowing it was true. It was still true. I ran my tongue over dry lips. All right, so I was gutless. For two cents I would, even now, just skip this whole frightening confrontation with my mother-in-law.

I shut my eyes. Mrs. Kinsolving . . . tall, short; thin, fat; ugly, pretty. There had never been time for pictures. Could I go on like this the rest of my life, watching her jump from one shape to another every time I closed my eyes? Could I go on hearing her say the lines I dreamed up for her, dreaming up lines of my own to say back so that sometimes I was aware that people were looking at me oddly, as if my lips had been moving?

I opened my eyes and looked into that mirror. The bus driver was looking at me. . . . Had I been moving my lips? I tried to look bright and normal, as if I took a sane interest in what he was saying. I played his words back, and they seemed to be something about a high-water mark.

"High-water mark," I said.

"Yes. Over there." He slowed the bus and pointed to a long, gray building where the land sloped down to the river's edge. "You can see how high the water came—there just above the first-floor windows—when they had the last flood."

"Last flood. Oh, yes." To that I was able to add a sensible comment: "I remember my husband saying he worked on something one summer that had to do with flood control."

"Yes. The situation's much better, but we still have floods. Had one last spring. This old couple drowned. People saw them on the roof as their house was swept downriver. They were supposed not to have spoken to each other for thirty years, and everybody wondered what, if anything, they said at the very end. . . ." He broke off and pointed to a sign at our right. It said, ALWAYS. DRIVE SLOW. POP. 81.

"Well, this is it." He took his hands from the wheel in a moment's inclusive gesture. "Always. Far from the madding and all that." He shifted gears, and we started climbing a little hill. "Once it wasn't such a bad little town—there was even a summer hotel here a few years ago. But the highway bypassed it, and now it's breathing its last."

It was a gray little town, huddling under magnificent tall trees. Cars rusted in weedy yards. Paint peeled on damp sidings. Two old men sat in chairs tilted back in front of a cavernous structure where a fading sign said, ALWAYS GARAGE. Fishing tackle was spread to dry on porches, and in the back of almost every house a sagging line of wash testified to many days of rain.

He held up his watch so I could see it, big, black-faced, set in the thick copper hairs of his wrist. "It's almost three o'clock. I go on down the river road to another little town

22

about twenty miles from here to pick up a couple of women who work the second shift at the mill. I'll be back here around five. Will you be wanting to go back?"

"Yes . . . yes." I told myself that two hours were nothing. At five o'clock I would be sitting on this bus again, and, whatever happened, it couldn't be worse than the worrying had been. I could glimpse the river again, a moving backdrop of blue beyond the gray houses. That big house was out there somewhere. Mrs. Kinsolving was out there. In minutes now I would be saying, "I am Francesca. . . ."

And Matthew's mother would say. . . .

I drew a thankful breath. It was no longer going to be necessary for me to try to imagine what Mrs. Kinsolving would say. Two hours from now I would have her words —burned on my brain, maybe—but they would have been said. I felt almost giddy in anticipation of my relief.

I looked at the coarse, red hair on the back of the driver's neck, at the tan collar beginning to fray a little. Coming back, I would sit right here in this seat behind him and talk and be very friendly no matter how many other people there were on this bus. He had been kind to me, and I was grateful. I liked nice, country boys with freckles on their ears, who were working their way through school. He would marry some nice girl, a nurse, no doubt, very big on maternal instinct. I hoped they would have crowds of beautiful children . . . Sheila, Monica, Patricia, Terence, Patrick, Leo. . . .

He was pointing. "Did you hear what I said? You can't see it from here for the trees, but the Kinsolving place is off the road that runs along the river, down there to our left. Their driveway is on the right. But the regular bus stop is just ahead, and if somebody is expecting you—"

It seemed simpler to let him think that somebody was expecting me.

He swung the bus up and around in a curve to stop in front of a diner that stood on a slight rise among trees. A sign said, RED AND WHITE CAFÉ. Years ago an indifferent hand had outlined windows, eaves, doors, with red paint. Somebody this year had put out red petunias, puny among exuberant weeds.

He said, "I call it the *Sad Café*. You know, *Ballad of the.* If you have to wait, it's safe to order a bottled drink. I do not recommend that you eat."

He jumped down off the bus, leaving the motor running, and turned back to hold up a hand to me. I was grateful to him for turning to look around in the other direction as I made my awkward descent.

He said, "I don't see that anybody's here yet to pick you up."

"Oh, I'm sure she will be right along. I'll just sit in there and wait where it's cooler." I turned and started walking toward the café, not wanting him to drive off and see me standing here like some Poor Pitiful Pearl. I looked back over my shoulder and said, "See you at five." And then, "You won't go without me, will you?"

"I won't." He gave me a grin, his teeth white and even. He swung up onto the bus that waited, shuddering. "Customers on this route aren't that easy to come by."

When the bus had gone noisily down the hill, the place was absolutely still. It was eerie, such stillness. Nothing moved except that river out there, not even the leaves on the trees. There weren't even any old people in sight now. It was as if everybody in the whole village slept.

In spite of the sluggish heat a chill went over me. I walked around puddles to the screen door, where a rusted

24

sign said, BONUS BUTTERMILK BREAD, and as I put my hand to the door, I looked back.

For a moment I had an almost overwhelming urge to run after the bus, calling, "Red—Red—come back, don't leave me!" He would see me in the rearview mirror. I knew he'd come back.

But the bus was disappearing down the river road.

Chapter 2

It was even hotter inside, heavy with the memory of hamburgers and French fries. There was a sour smell that was just as well not identified. A boy in a spotted apron stood behind the counter, and at first he seemed motionless, too, in some sort of trance. Then I saw that his thin shoulders jerked slightly and that his fingers made snapping motions.

Under his breath he sang along with a song that was turned low on the radio he wore in his shirt pocket. His jaw moved sideways: "I-hi still love you-hoo. Baby, deed I do-hoo. . . ."

The normality of it was a relief. I moved toward the counter and put my bag beside a pastry case that held pie and cake and doughnuts beaded with sweet sweat. Red had said it was safe to order a bottled drink. "I would like a Coke, please."

His eyes rested on me briefly without interest, slid down over my bulk, and then off to infinity. He moved to the end of the counter. "Baby, with those eye-hize . . . I jest ree-oh-lie-hize. . . ." Jerk, snap. "Large or small?"

"Large." What I wanted was water, but I was afraid to drink it here. A fly moved between the sweating doughnuts in the case. I eased up onto a stool in front of the counter, averting my eyes from the mess that was now visible.

"Glass?"

"I believe I'll just drink it from the bottle. You know, save dishwashing." I could see into the dishwater.

What can you tell me about Mrs. Matthew Kinsolving? I could imagine the indifferent lift there would be to the thin shoulders. He wouldn't have any interest in anybody over twenty. He reminded me of that boy who played C. W. Moss in *Bonnie and Clyde*. I guessed him to be about fifteen or sixteen.

He put the Coke in front of me, and I looked at the fog that drifted out of the open top. I took hold of the bottle, tilting it, watching the activated bubbles rising frantically. And then I lifted my head and smiled at him, aware that the only pretty thing left about me was my smile. I gave it all I had. "Tell me something . . . what's a swinger like you doing in a place like this?"

He stopped picking his chin, looked at me, saw me. "Sister, you said it. Man!" He reached into the pocket of his apron for a cigarette. He struck a match with his thumbnail, lit the cigarette, blew out two perfect smoke rings, and leaned toward me on the counter. It was as if my question had uncapped a carbonated drink. Words, frantic as those bubbles, rose, spilled.

"I come here to live with my grandmother—know what I mean? My mother gets herself married to this jerk with a whole bunch of little kids. So I, you know, come here. What else? I mean, my grandmother needs me. She's asleep back there, like every afternoon. She needs it, God, she's fifty. And I thought, well, you know, for the summer, the river and all that. And I thought, you know, maybe I could save up, buy me a jalopy, a motorbike, something, anything." He circled his hand. "But the place is dead. Nobody talks my language."

"I believe you." I did.

27

"There's only about five kids, maybe six, my age lives here. What I mean, these kids here don't know what life's all about. No, I mean that, they just don't know. Like, if I was to offer one of 'em a joint—or even a plain cigarette, fer cripe's sake—" He gave a bitter laugh.

"Why do you stay?" I pulled my watch around and looked at it. It was almost ten past three, and I had to get on with it, interesting as this conversation was.

"I'm not stayin'. Oh, no, not this cat, sister. I'm gonna get me a job in the city. I'm almost sixteen, man. I don't have to go to school no more."

"There's a school here?"

"Not anymore, there isn't. County school is all. Bus takes everybody. There was a school, and then it got washed out in the last flood. Man, that must of been a good one." He laughed hoarsely. "Know what I mean?"

I wasn't sure I did, but I gave him my attention.

"Cops drivin' up and down in the middle of the night. Sirens blowin'. Man, the place musta been alive then. Everybody had to move from the river road up to the church. Sleep there. I wish I'd of been here then. No school. Rats big as cats. That's what happens when there's a flood. The rats come out. Guy I know shot thirty in one night. That's when it's fun, when the rats come out."

"Groovy."

He leaned toward me again. "You're not from around here. I'd bet on that."

He meant it as a compliment, and I acknowledged it with another one of my great, big smiles. I had known there would be an opening, and I slid into it. "You're right. I'm not from around here. I'm going to be here for just about two hours, and I've got a feeling that'll be plenty, man. I came to see Mrs. Kinsolving."

28

"Her.'

"Yes."

He blew another smoke ring, poked his finger through the hole, and smiled at me. "Want to know something?"

"What?"

"If I was to of guessed who you come to see, it'd of been her."

"Why?"

"Oh, I don't know. Something about you."

"You mean I look like her?"

"Oh, hell, no. She's as old as my grandmother. White hair and all that. You kin to her?"

"Not really. Do you know her?"

"No. But I see her drivin' past every two, three days. That car. Man, what I wouldn't give. One of them old Lincolns. Black. Big. . . ."

I wasn't interested in talking about old cars. "What is she like, this Mrs. Kinsolving? I've never met her."

"Like?"

"I mean, is she friendly?"

He shrugged. "Oh, sure, I guess. She waves, like anybody else. Is she gonna pick you up?"

"No. I thought there'd be a taxi, maybe—"

"Used to be."

I sipped the last of my Coke. "I can walk. It's not too far, is it?"

"Well, no." His eyes went over me. "Hot for walking, but you can do it in ten, fifteen minutes if you take it slow."

I would take it slow. I put the money for my drink on the counter and added a tip. "I just go down this road that curves along the river, and then—"

"That's right. Look, you come over here to the window, and I'll show you. If it wasn't for all them trees, you could see the place real good."

I followed him to a window beyond some little tables, where he pulled aside red-checked curtains. Dust motes shimmered in the air. He pointed through tree branches, and I could see a small peninsula extending into the river, sickle-shaped, with the point curving back toward us, making a small bay. The end of the peninsula rose a little and was tree-shrouded. I couldn't see the main part of the house, but I could see a small, square tower rising above the trees, proudly aloof. It would have been impossible to have imagined anything less like the town of Always.

My heart sank. Matthew had never given me any indication that he had lived in a place like this.

I said, "It's like . . . a castle."

"Yeah. I never seen a castle."

"Maybe it's too far for me to walk down there and back. The road probably isn't very good for walking anyhow—" I looked at him almost hopefully.

"Shoot. That's not a bad road to walk on. It's downhill most of the way. And I bet you she'll give you a ride back up here in that big Lincoln."

It would have been so easy to have stayed right there and killed those two hours. I could have bought another drink, leafed through a magazine, talked some more to this boy whom I liked well enough—I always empathize with the losers. In view of the heat, the distance, my condition, it might even have been more sensible. But I had a strong feeling of now-or-never. And I was curious.

The walking didn't bother me. In the city I had walked miles during these past months to see all those movies. I was in good physical condition, and exercise was good for me—even that unhelpful little book told me that.

A cloud of gnats followed me down the hill, like an embodiment of all my worries, but I waved the gnats away and tried to forget the worries. The river was a swift and brimming blue, with boats and barges that seemed to move slowly. Distance may have lent some charm to the Kentucky shore over there, but here on this side there was anything but beauty.

A wharf leaned, rotting; tin cans and bottles lurked in the weeds at the sides of the road; the houses here slumped a little further into decay than those back up on the hill. One stood at a crazy angle, half off its foundations, and I thought of the last flood Red and the boy had mentioned.

I saw no one except for a young boy minding his business, fishing out at the end of the wharf. But a curtain twitched in a dingy window; voices, raised in loud argument, stilled suddenly as I walked past. *Look at that girl,* the imagined whisper followed me. *She's pregnant. Who is she?*

I was glad when I had passed the dozen or so houses and came to the mailbox on a stone pillar with the name Kinsolving. A sign had the words DEAD END: NO TRESPASSING. I turned in; the driveway curved so that I could not see all the way to the end of it. That was a relief. It would have bothered me to know that my mother-in-law might be watching me approach the house.

The driveway had been paved with cement once, but it was broken now, puddled and weedy in spots. There was evidence that the place had been landscaped at one time on rather a grand, parklike scale. There were stone benches placed here and there, flowering shrubs that didn't look wild, graveled paths. But the shrubs were in need of pruning, and the paths, some of them, led through swamps where cattails and wild blue iris now stood in water.

At one place the little peninsula narrowed, and the river lapped close on either side. The high, blue sky gave no sign of any more rain, but if just a few inches more had fallen during this last rainy week, the place would have been on an island, and I would have been blocked from going farther.

It pleased me to realize that my courage had risen. I was glad I had not come this far and found a barrier between me and Mrs. Kinsolving.

I passed a thicket of trees and saw on my left a rise of ground and on it . . . statues? No, it was a graveyard, small. I could see an iron fence around it. Matthew had mentioned the family graveyard once and said it used to scare him when he was a little boy. What else had he told me? I tried to remember every word, but only scattered bits came back.

I loved coming home summers after being away at school . . . Culver, Oberlin . . . I found a pearl one summer, a real, freshwater pearl . . . still there in my room if my cousin Kenny hasn't swiped it . . . he swiped a ring from me once, my grandfather's . . . head of a lion with a diamond in its mouth . . . he took a shell off a turtle once, and it died . . . cruel . . . my mother used to have to make me play with Kenny when he came . . . you'll like my mother.

Every time he had ever mentioned his mother to me he had ended with those words.

Sadly I thought that I already knew some things about Matthew's mother that he had not lived long enough to find out. She may have loved him; I believed she did, but that love had not been big enough to stretch to include me nor even Matthew's child. She must have known how badly I needed her when Matthew first died. I was glad I had waited to come here when I really didn't need her so much anymore.

I was beginning to be very tired now. The road just

ahead of me curved, and I could glimpse the wrought iron of big gates. I was sure that when I had gone through those gates, I would be in full sight of the house. It would be better if I sat to rest for a while. I could comb my hair.

There was one of those little stone benches not far from the path. Mud squished up over my toes as I made my way through tall grass to reach it. My watch said it was twenty minutes of four; I would give myself just ten minutes.

Gratefully, I sat on the stone bench and looked out over the river that I had always heard called the beautiful Ohio. It *was* beautiful; no wonder a song had been written about it. A little breeze had sprung up to ruffle my hair, to dry, a little, the sweat on my face. A boat horn sounded on the river and seemed to be answered by another. I tried without much success to imagine that Matthew had sat here, had bicycled along these paths, had climbed these big trees.

As always, whenever I sat quietly, I became conscious of the child. He bumped, moved crankily. I remembered the way Allegra used to sit, her hands spread over her stomach, glassy-eyed with pleasure. *Here, feel*—she had said to me once, forcing my young hand against her weirdly humping dress and holding it there.

Was that part of my hang-up? Oh, I was so tired of trying to figure myself out, tired of rationalizing. . . .

I held out my feet to see if the mud on them was too noticeable. It had been months since I had been able to reach my feet comfortably. From my bag I took a comb and ran it through my short hair, not needing to look in a mirror. I found a nail file and worked a little on the nails I had bitten.

Last summer my hair had been longer, and my nails had started to be a respectable length on that day when I went to Mexico with Matthew and held out my hand in that dark little shop to try on the lovely wide, handcrafted wedding rings. I remembered how pretty I had felt that day. Even my hair felt pretty, and I have always known I have ugly hair. But Matthew made me feel pretty all over. Loved . . . cherished . . . forgiven. . . .

Forgiven is a beautiful word. Somebody said once that it is the most beautiful word in the English language, and I know it to be so. I felt humble still at the thought of Matthew's forgiveness. One day on the beach before we went to Mexico, before I said I would marry him, I made him listen to the whole dreary story leading up to the day he had found me in the beach shack.

When I was eleven, I was in love with my father.

Let's leave Freud out of this.

He married Allegra. Laughing Allegra. Boarding school then for me, which they couldn't afford, but it was better than having me there looking at them. College. They had four kids and no money for me, so I got a partial scholarship to Merriam and bravely started working my way, ignoring the taunts of rich classmates. I carried trays, stuff like that. Don't cry now; it gets worse later.

It couldn't possibly. He was grinning at me.

I remembered looking at his grin and lying back on the sand, covering my eyes with my arm, not wanting to have to see his face when I told him the rest.

Listen, Math. I have to tell you the rest, and then if you don't want to marry me—

I don't want to hear.

You have to hear. There was this professor. I was in one of his lit classes. He was forty years old and very popular with all the beady-eyed little college girls. He was probably some kind of an authority on sex customs. You've heard about chastity belts, but did you know that at one

34

time, somewhere, they used to sew their ladies up before they went to war?

Grisly. Really?

Yes. The girls in the class would turn red, some of them, when he told us stuff like that.

Did you?

Me? Sure, I turned red. I was a virgin then. And it embarrassed me to know that he looked at me mostly when he got off on those kicks. He gave me a job typing, even though I typed with two fingers. I needed that job with almost no money ever coming from home.

I also needed to be touched, held, reassured that I was loved.

I put my head back against the tree trunk and shut my eyes now, remembering the way my breath came so fast and my voice sounded hoarse when I said, *I started sleeping with him.*

Here with my eyes shut it was easy to remember how it had been that day lying there on the sand, my eyes shut against the sun, against his eyes, my breath labored with unhappiness. When I started to say more, he put his hand over my mouth, and I pushed it away, spitting at the grains of sand. *No, Matthew, I have to finish telling you.*

Do you think, darling child, I've been a priest? Oh, Francesca, Francesca. I could tell you about a dozen girls, names, places . . . so just shut up.

I am a loser, Math. You don't want to get mixed up with me.

I want very much to get mixed up with you. I don't care what you did last year at Merriam College. I just care about what you're going to do this summer and next year and all the years of our lives. You were searching for a father image. Your father had rejected you. I understand, and I have heard all I want to hear.

35

Hush. You haven't heard the bad part. The professor had a wife. She was forty, too. When she found out about us, she killed herself. Yes, killed. With a gun. She left a note to somebody, and my name was in it. Nobody would have anything to do with me. I was expelled. It was the end of my scholarship, the end of everything. They wrote to my father. He had pulled a lot of strings to help me get that scholarship, and he wrote to me. He said, "Do not come back. I do not want these children even to know you." My voice broke.

Francesca, Francesca, don't.

Yes. So I ran away. I found this shack on the beach where nobody seemed to live. It was May. I thought I might write a novel—I used to get A's in composition. Death wishes up to my armpits and all that, I thought I would write the sad story of some girl like me, brave enough only to die. I never wrote one word. My money ran out. I tried to catch fish—that's how I got the fishhook in my hand, the blood poisoning. You know what I was like when you found me.

I opened my eyes now and looked at Matthew's river. He found me. Loved me. Forgave me. Married me. Got me with this child—yes, in that order. Our relationship had been proper; propriety was belatedly important to both of us because this was love, and it was for the rest of our lives.

We had one week of marriage.

And here I was now, alone on this bench, at this place where it must be true that he had lived. It was time for me to get up now and walk up that drive alone and knock at that door and say, "I am Francesca."

I looked at my watch. It was almost ten minutes of four. Yes, that was about right, leaving half an hour or so for a proper call on my mother-in-law. Oh, Miss Vanderbilt, sorry about no white gloves. I would have to go a bit heavy on the New England accent, broaden my *a*'s, a very proper Cabbot with two *b*'s. I was almost eager now to get on with it.

I got a little more mud on my sandals as I made my way to the driveway, but I wasn't going to worry about that. I wasn't going to worry about anything now. I held my head high and walked the way I had been taught to walk at Bewdley Hall. Pity I couldn't hold my stomach in.

The big, wrought-iron gates framed a view of the house. On a slight knoll, it rose three stories high, built of gray stone, almost completely covered with ivy except for the square tower which rose above the third floor. The tower had square, spaced stones along the top. Like gray teeth bared at the sky.

Ridiculous. I discarded the dramatic phrase which I knew I must have read somewhere. "Crenelated" was the word. That, too, was from something I had read, a poem, but I believed it was correct. The house was not really so overpowering. It was a scaled-down version of a Rhine castle admired on somebody's grand tour in the last century, that was all. At that time it very likely hadn't cost more than a few thousand dollars.

The driveway divided to circle the house. There was a flagstone walk to the front door. The house, now that I was almost within its shadow, hardly resembled a castle at all. It had more the look of a public building that had fallen into disuse. A courthouse; an old school; almost a prison.

Grass was growing out over the uneven stones of the flagstone walk, and ivy. I knew the ropelike vines would be strong enough to pitch me forward since my balance was precarious these days, so I walked with care, keeping my eyes on my feet. I did not intend to go sprawling here at Mrs. Kinsolving's door.

37

I went up the two shallow, broad front steps to a sort of terrace. Large ornamental stone jars on either side held weeds. From a distance the ivy had softened the lines of the house, seemed to cling lovingly. Here in the shade of the north side of the house, it had had a different look, was almost sinister. The main branches of the ivy were as thick as my wrists with a profusion of gray tentacles, like centipedes. They had crawled around windows, prying; they were reaching into the mortar between stones, loosening. Still another vine that I thought might be wisteria had pushed aside a gutter and waved thin, multiplying green fingers against the sky.

Ahead of me was the great front door. Iron-strapped, it had nailheads that had rusted, so that rusty stains trailed down over the gray, weathered wood. High up on the door, so high that I would have had to stand on tiptoe to see into it, was a small window of leaded glass. The door looked as if it had not been opened at all this summer. Tendrils of ivy, some of them almost a foot long, were growing out over the edges of the door.

I didn't know whether the door could be opened or not. I didn't know whether I ought to knock here or not. Very likely there were other doors around at the side or back. But I didn't intend to go looking for other doors.

My hand went out to the heavy iron knocker, which was shaped like the head of a lion. I hesitated, conscious of my fast-beating heart, the dryness of my mouth. I wet my lips, whispered, *Mrs. Kinsolving? I am Francesca.*

The knocker was very heavy. It creaked when I lifted it to tap twice. My tap was timid; I didn't want to make any great sound that would reverberate alarmingly through the house. Obviously Mrs. Kinsolving did not have very many callers who came knocking at this door.

Here in the shade it was almost cool. I waited, staring at

the door. I became conscious that my face wore what felt like a rather foolish, expectant smile, and I let it go, knowing that it was possible someone could be looking at me through that high, leaded window. I turned and looked out over the little bay that was visible here and there through the overgrown shrubbery and trees. I could not see the little town of Always, but for all its dreariness, I liked knowing that it was over there just across the bay.

I felt now quite definitely fond of that boy, that swinger, over at the Red and White Café. And it was a comfort to know that in just about an hour—only one blessed hour! —I would be on that bus with Red. Now that I thought about it, he really didn't look much like Albert Finney. He just looked like a helpful, friendly bus driver who was part of the ordinary, normal world I was going to be so glad to get back to.

For some reason my courage, even my curiosity, had ebbed a little. If she didn't come to this door pretty soon, I would think that she had watched me come up the drive and was looking at me now, maybe from one of those little balconied windows on the second floor, waiting for me to go away.

I listened. There was only the sound of the hurrying river, a whispering of the breeze through ivy, a slight twittering, as of sparrows among the leaves. No sound at all came from within the house.

Good. I took a deep breath. Nobody was at home. It was safe to knock again.

My hand was on the knocker when a cry came from the back of the house. Sudden, high-pitched, a keening sound. It rose again, followed by babbled sounds, half wept.

Frozen, I stood there, unable to move. That cry came again, piercing, sorrowful, not of this world. I took a backward step and then turned, stumbling. Oh, my God, don't let me fall! I watched my feet as I went down the steps, walking as fast as I could along the flagstones, fearing the ivy that seemed to clutch for my feet.

The end of the walk now. The open drive, the hot sun. I wished I dared run.

Back at the house there was a noise. It was a creaking, a groaning, and then a tearing sound of the ivy reluctantly letting go its hold on the door.

I walked faster, my straw bag knocking against my leg. No footsteps were following me. No voice called to me. I was afraid to turn and look back. I was afraid not to turn.

I turned. A tall woman had come out of the door and was standing on the terrace, looking at me. She had ivory hair. She wore a white dress.

Never let them know you are afraid. No, no, that was dogs you weren't supposed to let know. This was Matthew's mother standing there. I found myself moving back toward her, trying to remember the words I had come here to say.

"Mrs. Kinsolving?"

"Yes."

"I am Francesca."

She had eyes of a curious, pale gray, almost without color. They moved over me calmly. "Yes." And then she said in a voice that was flat and without modulation, "You came at an unfortunate time. It was necessary to drown the kittens."

I had reached the terrace now and stood just two steps below Mrs. Kinsolving. Those sounds came again, a mournful, wordless babbling in a lower key. Through the open door I could see a woman, a girl. She had tangled, dark hair, and she crouched back fearfully against the wall, her eyes on us.

The ivory head turned, following my gaze. "Kathleen

doesn't understand, of course. She had hidden one of them. But I followed the mother cat."

I steadied trembling fingers against my throat. "Kathleen? Kathleen is—"

"Feebleminded. Yes." She smiled at me now, her teeth strong and real and as ivory as her hair. She was a handsome woman, a Mother-of-the-Year type. "Oh, you mean *who* is Kathleen?" There was a pause. "Kathleen is Matthew's sister. Won't you come in, Francesca?"

Chapter 3

NUMB, I WENT into the dark, paneled hall. It seemed almost cold in here and very damp. A great, square staircase went up to a landing from the other end of this big hall. Stained glass at the landing shot the gloom with red . . . purple . . . gold. Big, old furniture loomed. Portraits stared at me from the walls. There was a musty, earthy smell, as of mushrooms growing.

The girl was nowhere to be seen now, but I felt that she crouched, peered at us through that hair from somewhere. Matthew's sister . . . feebleminded . . . God, please, no. . . . My child lurched within me.

Mrs. Kinsolving had closed the front door with some difficulty, and now she came past me and moved ahead, a stately woman, all that ivory hair neatly swirled to a bun in back. We passed a very large room on our right, where curtains were drawn. I glimpsed furniture shrouded in white dustcovers, like wraiths sitting quietly, waiting. Farther along the hall, also on the right was a smaller room, a library. She took me in there.

There was a big secretary, tall, with many pigeonholes and much visible clutter of papers and letters. Books, many hundreds of them on shelves that lined the room and went almost to the high ceiling. An Oriental rug, much worn, with rumpled places and threads that could catch an unwary foot.

I stepped carefully, sat carefully on the dark velvet chair she indicated beside a low table. The chair was too low for my comfort; I sat on the edge of it, my knees apart in that graceless, ninth-month position that let me breathe. My feet were planted firmly but tucked back a little so the traces of mud wouldn't show. My bitten nails were turned inward to my palms.

Not that my feet mattered now, nor my nails. Not that anything I had worried about mattered now. That face I had glimpsed. Those frightened, frightening sounds. Was it possible that I had misunderstood and that Mrs. Kinsolving had only seemed to say that girl was Matthew's sister?

She seated herself across from me stiffly, as if her knees pained her, saying something about her arthritis always being worse when it was going to rain. A pack of cigarettes lay on the table beside her. She took one, and in a voice that I now recognized as the voice of someone who was very deaf she said, "Would you like a cigarette?"

"No, I . . . thank you, no."

That smile again, those splendid teeth, her own. "So many of you young people seem to have stopped smoking these days. Or perhaps you have not ever taken it up?"

"I stopped. I do miss it. It is relaxing. I suppose I may start again—you know, afterward. . . ." I pressed my sweating palms against the dark velvet arms of the chair.

"Are you sure you won't have one now?"

"Yes. Thank you. Quite sure."

"It is very warm today outside. So humid after all the rain we have been having."

I said, Yes, it was humid. I got a tissue from my bag and blotted my face, my neck.

"Too warm today, really, for walking. You did walk—all the way from the village?"

"Yes. Yes, I did. I thought I would be able to get a taxi. But I have always walked a lot, especially lately. I like to walk." My voice had a foolish sound.

"And you are stopping at—"

"The Ar-something, the big motel on 52 where the road turns off to come to Always."

"Oh, I see." She exhaled, watching the smoke. "Yes. I understand that is a very good motel."

"Yes, it seems to be. Quite modern."

"How nice. And you came on the bus?" She turned to place the ash from her cigarette carefully in the ashtray beside her. "That dreadful bus. That tiresome old man—"

"He was young. He was just driving the bus for his uncle. Filling in. . . ."

I could be the Avon lady, I thought, about to reach into my bag for one of this month's specials now that the preliminary small talk was over. *Half price on our marvelous hormone cream, Mrs. Kinsolving. This month only. And with it, absolutely free . . . I stifled hysteria.*

I am Francesca—did you not hear me? Wife of Matthew, your dead son. I carry his child, your grandchild. Look at me. Recognize me.

I had imagined tears, hate openly expressed, accusations, but never this ignoring of all that lay between us, this talk of weather and buses and tiresome old men.

She was saying that the old man who usually drove the bus was quite a character and that the woman who ran the Red and White Café was a character, too. "We do have our share of characters around here!" She gave a laugh. "Did you have a chance to talk to her?"

"No. No, I didn't have a chance to talk to her. She was asleep, the boy said. He was working there, her grandson."

"A boy. Oh, yes. I believe I have seen him around there lately. Well, now, let me see. May I offer you a glass of lemonade?

"No, thank you.'

"Are you sure? I drink quite a bit of lemonade—lemons, you know, are supposed to be very good for arthritis. But that may be an old wives' tale. How about a nice glass of iced tea with mint? We have our own mint. Kathleen could get it for us. Anything simple, Kathleen does quite well."

"No, really." And then I said, "I thought Matthew was an only child. He never told me he had a sister."

"No." She tucked back a strand of pale hair and adjusted a hairpin. "Matthew never knew about Kathleen. He was only two when she was born. We put her into a special home when she was just a few months old and then into a school. There seemed no reason for him to know he had a sister like that. But the school was very expensive, and last September I found it necessary to bring her here."

"Was it a—a birth injury?"

She put out her cigarette. "Yes. Yes, it was a birth injury." She smiled at me warmly. "Perhaps a glass of water?"

"Yes, thank you. I believe I would like some water if it isn't too much trouble."

She left the room. I got up and walked around, feeling that I must search for reality, something I could hang onto and believe was true. Had I made some stupid, harebrained mistake and come to the wrong house? I touched books, not seeing their titles. Was it possible that she was really Matthew's mother? Had she even heard me when I said I was Francesca?

At the window I widened the space between heavy draperies and looked out through trees across a tangled lawn

45

that sloped to the river. Was this just one of my vivid dreams? No, I could never have dreamed anything like this woman with her hollow voice, her eerie courtesy. How was it possible for her to so totally disregard all that we were to each other, all that had happened? She had not even made any mention of my pregnancy.

Something moved against my leg, startling me. I looked down and saw the mother cat, a fawn and brown Siamese, swollen with milk. She made hoarse, calling noises, looking behind the long draperies for her drowned babies, under the chairs, under a large cabinet that held curios. I had to look away.

That girl's voice again out in the back somewhere, making a gibberish of unintelligible sounds. I heard Mrs. Kinsolving say sharply, "Enough, Kathleen!" In a moment she came back into the room with a glass of water for me.

I drank nearly all of the cold water and handed the glass back to her. She looked toward the cat who was continuing her agitated search out in the hall and said easily, "Our Siamese mated with an alley cat. The kittens were no good . . . as is always true of any species when a thoroughbred mates with a mongrel." Her eyes moved over me, came back to my face. And then almost instantly, as if to deny any intended slur in her words, she gave me that big, brilliant Mother-of-the-Year smile, held it.

I turned back to the window, my head high, hoping my color would not rise. But she could not hurt me; I disliked her too much. *Five minutes more,* I thought, *and I will get out of this house.* I kept my eyes on the river. "Mrs. Kinsolving, I wrote to you. I wrote to you twice. I have wondered if you got my letters."

She was sitting down again. "I must ask you to turn and face me when you speak. Since my illness, I have been

46

very deaf. I do have a hearing aid which I wear sometimes, but the noises distract me and I prefer reading lips."

I sat across from her in the low chair and said distinctly, "When were you ill?"

"Last summer." She reached for another cigarette. "I was ill when the letter came from my son saying he was getting married. He was to have spent his last leave here with me. I had looked forward to it for a very long time. That boy was my life. That letter from him nearly destroyed me."

Oh. So it was hate after all. Courteous, well-bred, but hate. I didn't need to find out any more. I would not bother to mention again the letters I had written her—I had some dignity, too—but I felt I should say in defense of Matthew: "He did try to call you when he got his sudden orders. But he was told that the phone had been disconnected."

"Our small local telephone company had always given us unsatisfactory service—Matthew was aware of that—and with my sudden hearing loss it was almost useless."

"He did worry over not being able to talk to you."

"Indeed. But he did not worry enough to come and make sure I was all right."

We were on the verge of quarreling. I said helplessly, "There was so little time. He wrote you and explained all that. And I wrote. . . ." I stopped, remembering I had decided not to mention my letters.

She toyed with the cigarette, turned it, studied it. Her eyes when they lifted to look at me again were as pale as moonstones. "I received your letters, of course. Most brides would have waited for their mother-in-laws to write to them first."

I opened my mouth, closed it; I could think of abso-

47

lutely nothing to say. The reason for my coming here seemed hard to remember. What was it I had said to Miss Gee?

"I confess I was astonished to see you here today. I never dreamed that you would come uninvited."

I reached down and picked up my bag, glanced at my watch. It was exactly four thirty.

I said, "I must go." I found that I was smiling, too. The Avon lady who doesn't make a sale but smiles anyhow.

"Oh, you must not feel that I am sorry you came. I shall give you dinner. There are many things which we must talk about, now that you are here."

My astonishment must have shown. "Oh, thank you. I couldn't think of it. My bus—"

"That bus? Oh, no, no, I will not hear of it!" Her flat voice was cordial. "I shall insist on giving you dinner. And then, after dinner, I shall drive you to the motel where you are staying. My car is quite comfortable."

I had no intention of staying in this house for dinner. I was much too tired for more of this stupid pretending. "How kind of you, Mrs. Kinsolving. But the bus driver has already promised to wait for me. I had no intention of making more than a short call anyhow. If you should want to drive me to the village—"

"How ridiculous." Her laughter had the same empty sound as her voice. "Really preposterous when you have come all this long distance to see me. I am from Kentucky, as Matthew may have told you, and we pride ourselves on our hospitality."

"I am sure you do." My sweetness was just as fake as hers. "I really cannot stay."

"Let me think," she said, as if I had not spoken. "There is a canned ham, I believe, very nice on a hot night. I can make us a salad—we have a small garden out in back with

48

our own lettuce and radishes. Poor Kathleen, she does so enjoy working in our little kitchen garden. Beaten biscuit. But then perhaps you have never had beaten biscuit, being from New England?"

I stared into the moonstone eyes. The unreality again. I had to get away from it. "I cannot stay, Mrs. Kinsolving. It is quite impossible. I'll just go along now. I like to walk. I would really much prefer to walk. And there will be plenty of time for me to make my bus if I start now."

I stood up so quickly that a wave of dizziness went over me. I clutched for the back of a chair.

"There, now, you see!" The quick hand she put on my arm was warm, almost kind as it steadied me. I looked into the pale eyes. No, not kind.

"I really cannot allow you to go now. I am a nurse—did Matthew never tell you that?"

"No, I don't think so—" I really was feeling a little ill.

"Well, I am, and it is quite obvious to me that you have overestimated your strength. You should have known better than to have tried to walk all that distance in that terrible heat and humidity this afternoon. You must stay here now, rest for a while before dinner. We eat around seven. Come this way. The rooms upstairs are not used, not ready, of course, for a guest. But you may lie down in my room. It is right back here on this floor. Come, I will show you."

We were in the hall. Her hand stayed on my arm. I still felt a little light-headed, and I was letting her guide me. The colored glass at the turn of the stairs flashed a brilliant red . . . purple . . . gold. And that was the only warmth.

Bewilderment took hold of me. How could the Matthew I had known ever have thought I would like this woman with the strange, cool eyes? How could he ever have felt close to her? How could he ever have lived in this house?

49

I could not visualize him ever sliding down this banister, ever running in this big hall and disarranging these Oriental rugs.

Surely, by some coincidence unimaginable to me now, I had made a mistake. I had come to the wrong house.

Suddenly, I saw his face. I gasped, stopped, looked right into Matthew's eyes.

Chapter 4

I LET OUT the breath I had been holding. No, the painted eyes were not quite so bright; the hair was worn a different way. The man in the big, gold-framed portrait was young; he wore a wide-lapelled suit and a bright, red tie. The artist had not been a very good one—the flesh tones were too ruddy, the mouth too red and pretty. But Matthew's mouth had curved that same way, and his hair had been this same warm brown.

She had stopped to stand beside me. "Matthew's father, of course. I see you are struck by the resemblance. There was quite a remarkable likeness between father and son." She straightened the heavy frame and moved to the next portrait. "This was his father's sister."

I saw a girl with dark hair that curled around her face. The style of the dress was what I imagined styles to have been twenty years ago. Again, there was a picture-postcard brightness to the colors, but the smiling red mouth was happy.

"Was she the mother of Kenny?"

"Kenny?"

"Matthew mentioned a cousin Kenny once—"

"Oh, no, no." She straightened that frame, too. "This

51

poor girl never married at all. She died just a short time after this portrait was painted."

I moved my eyes away. It hurt to look at those happy, dead eyes. But I was beginning to get the feeling that Matthew had, after all, lived in this house, to feel close to him. I wasn't going to mind staying here a little while longer.

Mrs. Kinsolving led the way along a short wing to the right, just off the wide main hall. I had a brief glimpse of Kathleen's peering face as a door to the right was drawn shut. Mrs. Kinsolving was opening a door to the left.

"This is my room. It has its own small bath right here, which will be convenient for you."

The room was dark. The windows were closed, and the shades were drawn. I thought surely she would open them to let in a little fresh air, but she told me that since the room was on the south, she never raised the shades nor opened the windows until the sun had gone down. She turned on a shaded light beside the bed—big, like the one Lincoln slept in—and she turned on a floor fan. The still, hot air moved a little.

There was an Indian-print spread on the bed. She believed I would find what I needed by way of towels, washcloths, and soap on the bathroom shelves. She checked the bathroom and did some arranging. When she came out, she glanced at my feet. If I could just wash the mud off my feet, she said I could lie down on her bed. She gave me another of her big smiles, hoped I could sleep. And was gone.

Why not? I stared at the door when it clicked shut, repressing a hysterical desire to laugh wildly. Any girl with no more sense than to have allowed herself to be insulted and then led in here like some docile animal would be perfectly capable of washing her feet, lying down, and going to sleep instantly.

52

The bathroom was all tiled whiteness with pink towels. I took off my dress and scrubbed, using a lot of soap and water. After I had sat on the edge of the tub and washed my feet, I put my ugly tan tent back on and combed my ugly tan hair. I leaned then to look at my face. With these tan spots of pregnancy I looked like some new kind of animal.

Her words about thoroughbreds mating with mongrels came back. Had she actually meant . . . ? Yes, I believed she had. Would you have me then *drown* the baby, Mrs. Kinsolving?

I cleaned my teeth with one of the pink washcloths. Unsatisfactory, but better than nothing. I really must remember to send her a copy of Father's book about the Cabbot family if he ever finished it. Maybe I should tear the homecoming page out of my college annual and send her that? My college board scores? It was obvious that she thought I lacked brains along with everything else.

I gave myself a big, toothy smile, feeling again a little giddy, a little removed from it all. *Normally, I am stunning, Mrs. Kinsolving. I can tell you've been wondering.*

Maybe I am in shock, I thought. Nothing serious. It is just that all this has been too much for Poor Pitiful Pregnant Pearl. Unhinged her mind. I found a brush under the sink and scrubbed the mud off my ugly sandals.

Listen. I went into the bedroom then and turned off the light and lay down on her bed and cried. I had thought I was all through crying. I told myself I was crying about Red coming to the café and not finding me there—that seemed a safe thing to cry about. But there hadn't been anything I could do about it. I had been too tired to walk back. Perhaps as a nurse, Mrs. Kinsolving had seen that I was on the verge of exhaustion.

I got a tissue from my bag and blew my nose and lay

back again. I thought about her being a nurse and wondered why Matthew never had mentioned it, but there had been a million things we never got time to mention. For a minute I wondered why he had never said anything about her deafness until I remembered that she said it had come on her suddenly.

What, exactly, had Matthew ever told me about her? He had said her first name was Maria, that she was from the Bluegrass region of Kentucky, that she was fond of books. It all added up well enough except for the words: "You'll like my mother."

He never had qualified that by saying, "You'll like my mother, but. . . ." The "but" would have come without doubt if things had worked out so that he could have brought me here to meet her. He might have said then, "You'll like my mother, but she's jealous . . . but she thinks no girl on earth is good enough for me."

I turned restlessly on the bed, trying to get comfortable. I remembered that while I was still recovering from the blood poisoning, he told me he had written her about me and that he had received a very nice letter. I never saw that letter. If I had seen it, I might very well have been able to read things between the lines that a loving, uncritical son had not been aware of. Or it was possible that at that time she had put me in the category of some hurt, homeless puppy that he had been kind to. No threat.

Was there even a possibility that she really was not so bad after all? That she'd had a change of heart after those hurting things she had said to me? Did her insistence on my staying to have dinner with her mean that she intended to treat me decently, for Matthew's sake? Might it not be possible for the two of us to work out some sort of friendly enough relationship—never a very warm one—but with occasional letters, gifts at Christmas?

54

Never.

But I was not sorry I had come. It was behind me now, or nearly, and I would not have to wonder about her anymore.

Kathleen . . . yes, the sight of her had disturbed me, although I'd barely glimpsed her face. Thank God Mrs. Kinsolving had told me her difficulty was caused by a birth injury. A nurse; she would know about such things.

How odd that she never had let Matthew know about Kathleen. But, as she had said, that boy was her life. Very likely she had not wanted another child, so that it had been easy to reject her, put her away. She had certainly proven she was capable of rejecting me and my child.

The baby kept kicking crossly, as if unable to get himself comfortable, and I kept moving on the bed, trying to accommodate myself to the demands of my tenant. I was feeling more relaxed about him now, more certain of what my course should be. Tomorrow when I saw Miss Gee, I would tell her that my mind was made up about the adoption. I might even give her a brief account of this crazy encounter with my mother-in-law. Although I had spent only a short time at the agency yesterday, there had been a warmth there that I would be glad to return to.

"I am Miss Gee," she told me when I first met her. "It is spelled *G-e-e,* as in whiz." The little joke, I thought, to put me at my ease. In case workers' school they were probably taught that they should tell gentle little jokes to the unmarried mother and other unfortunates who must give their babies away. Pretty Miss Gee with real pearls in her ears and no wedding ring on her finger.

Didn't she need to be touched and loved and held close? And if she didn't have that need, how could she know us or get inside our skins enough to help us?

I fell asleep, wondering about Miss Gee. It seems amazing to me now that I was able to sleep there on Mrs. Kinsolving's bed, with the fan barely stirring that hot, heavy air.

I dreamed. In my dream I was getting married. I seemed to know that it was Kenny Kinsolving I was marrying, the cruel cousin who had taken the shell from the turtle, but I had not been able to see his face. My father was there to give me away. There were stained-glass windows that hinted at the colors of red, purple, gold. And many strangers stood close to me with bright, cold smiles on their faces.

I kept trying to see Kenny's face, but his head was bent low over the ring he was putting on my finger. It completely covered the gold ring Matthew had put there. And when I held up my hand to look at it, I saw that my new ring was made of tortoise shell.

I turned and ran, unable to scream. Big hands clutched for me, Mrs. Kinsolving's hands. They almost caught me, but I was able to pull myself free. I saw that it was this big stone house I was running in, not knowing my way, up one dark, winding corridor after another. The strangers were running after me, crying my name: "Francesca . . . Francesca . . ." with babbling echoes. I went on and on, blindly. There was a humming sound now and no light at all.

I woke in terror, my heart pounding, and sat up in the humming darkness, unable at first to think where I was. Oh. Oh, yes. It was only that fan over there that made the humming sound. I turned on the light by the bed, and the disturbing dream began to recede. I looked at my watch; it didn't seem possible that it was almost a quarter of seven. I yawned, feeling better. I must have been more tired than I realized to have slept almost two hours.

Red would have gone long ago. I was sure he had waited

for me at the Red and White Café. I was sorry about that. Maybe he would always wonder about me. And I would certainly always remember him. A nice, kind guy. Full of the milk of, as he would have said.

I slipped my feet into sandals which were still damp. I must hurry now. Put on some lipstick, comb my hair again, powder the brown spots to take away the mongrel look. I must brace myself to get through the meal with some dignity in that big formal dining room I had glimpsed opposite the drawing room. There would be the beaten biscuit, that smile. The family silver. Forks weighing half a pound apiece. . . .

But we ate with worn, brassy-tasting, plated silver, and the dishes must have been those she used every day in the kitchen. I sat at one end of the long, oval table, and Mrs. Kinsolving sat at the other. I noticed that she had a button in her ear now with a cord that disappeared in the front of her dress. I also noticed that there were glass-fronted cabinets holding fine china, thin crystal. I hadn't a doubt but that the real silver was in those many drawers.

I was irked no end. It really wasn't very clever of her, nor necessary. Apparently she thought that if she used her nice things, I might get ideas. But I didn't want her silver or her china or anything else. I wasn't grabby. Even Allegra, who would have told you readily enough that I was hateful and a brat, would have had to admit that I was not grabby.

We had ham, sliced very thin, a salad of mixed greens, and some flat, hard little things which, I supposed, were the beaten biscuit. But they were very good; I ate four. For dessert there was stewed rhubarb, which I would have enjoyed if I could have eaten it with a silver spoon.

During the meal I had just one uneasy glimpse of Kathleen through the door that led to the kitchen. She seemed badly coordinated. No mention was made of her eating with us or not eating with us. I could not help being relieved that she was not at the table. The meal was difficult enough without having that poor girl here with us, spilling, as she would almost certainly have done, and making those strange sounds which didn't quite seem to be words.

From the beginning it became obvious that Mrs. Kinsolving was not bothering with the fake graciousness that she had affected from time to time this afternoon. She ate very little, and I did not see the Mother-of-the-Year smile at all.

I tried some questions: How long had Matthew's father been dead? Ten years. Had Matthew ever attended the local schools at all? For a short time. Was he born in this house? Of course. A time or two I saw her reach into the front of her dress to adjust the battery of her hearing aid, as if she wanted to be sure she understood everything I said, but the answers she gave me were as short as possible.

When I asked when the house was built, she told me it was over a hundred years old. "Why are you so curious?"

"Curious? I'm sorry." I asked no more questions. It had seemed only polite to make a little conversation. Actually, I cared about nothing except finishing this meal and getting out of here. I sat very straight, a proper Cabbot with two *b*'s.

When she had put down her knife and fork and placed her napkin beside her plate, I did the same with a sigh of such relief that I was sure she must have heard it. I watched her, waiting for my cue to rise.

"One moment. I am sure you must have wondered why I did not answer your letters."

"Yes."

She lit a cigarette and rested her elbows on the table. "I did not answer your letters because I did not intend to recognize you as Matthew's wife."

I lifted my head and held it high, alert to the change that had come into her face, her voice.

"I hoped, quite frankly, that I would never have to see you. I assumed—foolishly, it seems—that you would have some reticence, some sensitivity. I was sure that any girl my son would choose for a wife would understand, by my silence, that I wished to be alone with my grief."

I tried to find words. I was too proud to mention my own grief. "Mrs. Kinsolving—you were his mother—it seemed that I couldn't just *not* try to—"

She held up her hand. "Let me say what quite obviously has to be said, now that you have been bold enough to come. There is no money. This place is mortgaged for more than it is worth. No buyer in his senses would make an offer for a run-down old house on the edge of a dying town. High water at times cuts us off from the shore."

The taste of that brassy spoon was in my mouth. "Mrs. Kinsolving, please understand . . . I do not want, do not need any money. I have my allotment. My father is—" the words stuck a little in my throat, "quite able to help me. I shall manage very well."

"I am sure of it." She said it dryly. And then, "What are your plans for the child?"

I told her I had already discussed the possibility of adoption with someone at an agency in Cincinnati.

Her pale eyes flicked up, then down. She rearranged her silver, positioned the water glass, studied it as if she might be deliberating a chess move. "That is the only thing to do, of course. Have the child adopted." She paused. "I advise you not to make any mention of the name Kinsolving."

59

"Why not?"

"The family is too well known in this state."

"But the records are always confidential. The parents who get the child will not know—"

"No, no. I am telling you not to mention the name to the adoption agency. The family taint is too well known."

"The . . . taint?"

"Yes. You have seen Kathleen."

"But you said—" My voice rose. "This afternoon you told me that Kathleen had a birth injury—"

"So I did." She touched each corner of her mouth carefully with her napkin. "One gets in the habit of covering up. But in this instance—between us—the facts do not need to be prettied. And they are not pretty, not at all. There was one uncle who was defective in the Kinsolving family. There were two cousins that I know of. One was so severely deformed that he was what, medically, is referred to as a monster."

My lips felt bloodless. "Then . . . you are saying . . . nobody will want. . . ."

"No, no, I am not saying that at all. I say only that you must not mention the family name. Kathleen looked perfectly normal at birth. I believe she tested normal. No doubt your child will actually *be* normal." She drew on her cigarette and said as she exhaled, "Or *is* it Matthew's child?"

I was speechless for seconds. "Not . . . not Matthew's child. Oh! How can you ask me such a question!"

"How can I?" She gave a short, unpleasant laugh, looking down at her silver, which she moved again. "I know considerably more about you than you think I do. I know the ugly reasons why you were expelled from Merriam College. I know about the professor at that college. I

60

know about that poor creature, his wife. I know that she killed herself.

Denial was useless. I whispered, "How—"

"Matthew told me." She said it harshly and waited for the blow to find its mark. She was breathing hard now, her color high. "Matthew. My son and I were always very close. He wrote to me. He told me all about everything. My son must have understood, if you did not, why I never wrote again."

The room seemed to darken. I had never fainted. I would not faint now. I took hold of the edge of the table, and a fork slid to the floor. "I do not believe you."

She shrugged. "I have kept his letter. I know about how he found you, a beach bum. How, like a fool, he took you to a hospital. I know that somehow you tricked him into marrying you. I know all that any mother needs to know about the girl her son married. Have you finished eating?"

I fumbled for my bag on the floor and got up. I followed her into the big hall, past the stairs toward the back of the house. A door led through a smaller hall, and we came out on a broad terrace, similar to the one at the front of the house. White roses grew on a trellis, sweet-smelling, heavy. The sky had clouded over, but the last rays of the sun slanted across my face.

Steps led down into a sort of courtyard, which was paved with cobblestones. There were several buildings ahead of us, built of gray stone like the house. One of them had a great, yawning door. As we approached, I could see the Lincoln inside, black, and I followed her through the yawning door.

She got in under the wheel, and I got in on the other side. Neither one of us said anything.

My hands were sweating, trembling. I wiped them on

my skirt, and I thought: In minutes now I shall be away from this house and this woman forever. I shall be back at that motel on the highway, where the room is modern and bright. There is an orange, plastic backrest on the bed. The television set has a remote-control button. I shall sit mindlessly on that bed and hold that button in my hand and look at the screen with the sound turned up loud. I shall try not to think. Not about Matthew, not about this child, not about Kathleen, not about this woman. When the last late, late show has gone off, I shall sleep. And then tomorrow. . . .

I would not let myself think about tomorrow.

She fumbled to locate the car key on the ring. She turned on the ignition. There was a grinding noise and a faint chug. And then nothing. She turned the ignition key again. This time there was only a grinding noise.

I turned to look at her. Her face was red, her foot to the floor.

For a minute we just sat there. And then she leaned to the ignition key again, stamping on the gas pedal as if it were some animal she might be trying to kill.

Nothing.

She straightened, smoothed back her ivory hair with both hands, breathing hard.

"Mrs. Kinsolving?"

She did not seem to hear me.

I saw that the button to her hearing aid had been pulled out of her ear. I touched her arm, and when she was looking at me, I mouthed the words carefully, hoping she could read my lips in the dimness. "It is still light enough for me to walk."

In her expressionless voice she said, "What nonsense. Of course you will not walk. I have flooded the engine, that is all. I shall wait for a few minutes and then try again. It will start. But the fumes of the gasoline are unpleasant—go back over there, and wait in one of the chairs on the terrace."

I went and sat in an old cypress chair on the terrace near the kitchen door. Beyond the row of low stone buildings I could see a path that led through weeds to a vegetable garden. I could see a larger building, a barn, and beyond it, the river. Everything was bathed now in the red light of sunset: the river; the roses; me. It was a strange light. I didn't like it.

A sudden breeze from the river, warm and heavy, wafted the smell of gasoline toward me to mingle it sickeningly with the scent of white roses. Some minutes passed . . . three? . . . five? I heard her trying to start the car again.

Inside, there were dishwashing sounds. But from time to time there would be a silence, and I felt that the girl Kathleen had come to stare at me from the kitchen door. I sat motionless, not turning around to look. I thought I might start screaming if I had to sit here much longer.

I lost track of the times that woman out there tried to start the car. She seemed to be working at something now under the hood. But the light was beginning to fade, and I thought the breeze smelled of rain. I knew panic. She wasn't going to get that Lincoln to run tonight, although I was sure she was every bit as anxious to have me go as I was to leave.

I started walking. Slowly, but with my breath coming hard. It was necessary to watch my feet because these rounded cobblestones here in the courtyard were treacherous. I was safely past the yawning door now, past the cobblestones. But the uneven places on the driveway must be watched, too. The light was going fast, and I must take no chances on falling.

How long had it taken me to walk to this house this afternoon? Fifteen minutes? . . . twenty? It would take me longer now. It would be black dark before I got to the river road and started up that last slope to the Red and White Café. I knew if I fell there, I could cry for help. That boy, somebody, would hear me. I knew that there would be no more buses tonight, but I was sure I could find someone to take me. I would pay well—ten dollars, twenty, anything—to get back to that motel on 52 tonight.

"I shall not let you go." The hollow voice came clearly.

I turned and looked back, and Mrs. Kinsolving stood there with a wrench in her hand.

"I quite literally will not let you go, Francesca. You could fall. If you fell, you almost certainly would bring on labor, and then where would we be?"

I clutched my bag against me, looking into the pale eyes which were absolutely without color as she came toward me in the dusk. There was almost a return now to this afternoon's cold civility. She said, "I am surprised that you would start off like that."

"I can walk. I would rather."

"Are you a fool then?"—she said it coolly—"in addition to everything else?"

I closed my eyes for a moment. I had the most awful feeling of being under some sort of spell. Those eyes. . . .

"The road leads through swamp—don't you remember? There are snakes this time of year. I do, after all, feel some responsibility toward you."

I said, "I am afraid it is going to rain. I can't take chances. You said sometimes you were marooned—"

"Nonsense. We never have floods in June."

She took hold of my arm and kept talking to me as if she felt she had to calm me. "The car will start in the morning. This has happened before. The battery is low. In warm weather it recharges itself during the night. And if it does not start, Kathleen will go to the village and take a note to the garage. We have a perfectly adequate garage in Always. One of the men will come out. There is no problem. You will sleep here tonight."

And so I let her take me back into that house, past the white roses, ghostly now in the dusk. Francesca, the Gutless, Mindless Wonder.

Chapter 5

In the big hall she said, "Sit here and wait," and I sank onto a carved, wooden, high-backed bench against the wall just outside the door of the library. She turned on the light and said, "I shall get Kathleen to help me get one of the bedrooms ready." She went along a narrow passage toward the kitchen, where dishwashing sounds had been resumed.

I put my head back against the bumpy carving and closed my eyes, feeling weak and bewildered. I despised myself for letting her control me, and I knew she must despise me, too. But what could I have done that I had not tried to do? She had meant it when she said she would not allow me to leave. I knew it would have been possible for her to restrain me physically. It would have been utterly senseless for me to have started out in the dark—I knew that—but how could I bear to spend a night in this house?

She came past me again. I said, "I would like to sleep in Matthew's room." But she continued on past, and I knew that she had not heard me.

I hurried after her and caught her arm. "Mrs. Kinsolving, I want to sleep in Matthew's room—"

She disengaged my fingers and looked at me coldly. "No, that is not convenient."

"I will never be in this house again—I promise you that. Let me sleep in Matthew's room."

"His room is upstairs. It has not been cleaned. We do not go upstairs."

"I don't care whether it's been cleaned or not! If you will get me some sheets, I can put them on. What possible difference can it make to you?" My voice was high-pitched, and I had to struggle for control.

Her pale eyes were on my face, as if she weighed the risk of hysteria. She turned away. "Go back and sit on the bench, and do try to calm yourself. I shall go upstairs and get the room ready, since you are so insistent." She raised her voice and called, "Kathleen! What is keeping you?"

Kathleen came, drying her big, red hands on the front of her dress. The dress was dark gray, with an institutional look. Her eyes darted toward me, and there was a half smile, uncertain, childlike. She walked with that stumpy, uncertain gait which you see sometimes in those who must be led by the hand.

They went up the stairs with Kathleen following her mother. Mrs. Kinsolving took them one at a time as if her knees hurt, as if she resented every step.

The bench was hard. The back was at a cruel angle, and the carving was bumpy so that it hurt my head when I leaned back. I sat there dully, dazed by my discomfort, but not wanting somehow to go into one of the dark rooms and look for a chair that might have been more comfortable. The portraits hung just opposite me under the carved balustrade of the stairs. I closed my eyes, not wanting to look at happy, dead people.

Matthew, I thought, *how could you have told her about me?* I wished I knew how his letter had phrased all that ugliness. Not unkindly, I knew him. But I wished I had never come to this house. I wished I never had seen Kathleen.

It had seemed so right to come! I remembered being convinced that it was the one thing I had to do before I could start liking myself. Was I, as Mrs. Kinsolving had said, a fool in addition to everything else?

Yes. I was a fool.

"Your room is ready now." She was calling me from somewhere upstairs.

It had taken a very long time.

Slowly, conscious of the weight of my child, I climbed the carpeted stairs, hauling myself along by clinging to the banister. At the top I came into a large hall like the one below. There were more portraits up here, badly hung so that they tilted forward rather alarmingly. These faces were of an older era, sober-looking, as was more fitting to that time, but I didn't have any interest in knowing who they were.

There were several closed doors off this hall. To my left, as downstairs, there was a wing with other doors. Mrs. Kinsolving stood near the end, waiting beside a door that was open on the right.

Kathleen came out of that room as I reached it, stumped past me, glancing at me uncertainly over an armload of trash that looked as if it might have come from desk drawers. A full wastebasket sat just outside the door, and Mrs. Kinsolving had another one in her arms.

It crossed my mind to wonder if it had been difficult for her to clean out Matthew's room—obviously for the first time. Or was all the grief past, overlaid by her hatred of me? And if so, did her hatred make grief easier to bear?

She waited as I looked around. It was a masculine room; there was a large, double bed, which looked as if it were brass or some kind of metal, painted tan to match the woodwork, the walls, the rug. A heavy, plaid spread, maroon and blue and tan, covered the bed. I saw a desk, large, flat-topped, with many drawers and a green-shaded lamp, hanging low. On the walls there were pictures, a gun rack with three guns, an Oberlin pennant and one for Culver, the big *C* swallowing the rest of the word. The side of the room next to the desk was all shelves which held many books, an alarm clock, a portable radio. One of the shelves held a shell collection and pieces of driftwood.

His room, no doubt about that. Matthew had been beachcombing when he found me.

I set my bag down on the big desk and went to the shell collection. I picked up one of them and saw a label in his handwriting. Without thinking I said, turning to her, "There was a pearl that Matthew told me I could have."

"There are no pearls." She said it flatly. "There are no jewels. There is nothing left that is of any value. I have told you that."

My temper snapped. With my accent so Bostonian it was about ten miles out in the Atlantic I said, "I know you told me that, Mrs. Kinsolving. The pearl had no value—Matthew told me it was only a freshwater pearl that he found when he was a little boy. You must know about it. But since you don't like me, and I don't like you, let's let it go, shall we?"

She lifted her chin, looking quite a bit like the headmistress at Bewdley Hall. "I know nothing about any pearl." She turned. Her dignity made my outburst seem childish. "You will find the bathroom at the end of this hall—I shall leave the light on. I have put out soap, towels. Kathleen, after her fashion, has cleaned it."

"Thank you."

"In the middle drawer of that chest you will find some

of Matthew's pajamas which I think you can wear. If there is anything else you need, I can send Kathleen up. I shall not attempt to climb these stairs again tonight."

"I won't need anything."

She closed the door.

I thought: *Up to now she has won them all.* And then I thought: *Oh, Matthew, why did you tell her?*

I glanced around at the walls; if there had been any personal pictures, they had been removed. I opened a desk drawer; it was empty. There wasn't the smallest scrap of paper. I opened all the others, and they were empty, too. How strange of her to have taken all this time to clean out these drawers. I wondered if she had found the pearl. I remembered that when Matthew was telling me about it, he had said, "It must be one helluva job for an oyster to make a pearl. But I guess maybe it's better than lying suffering with a rock in your eye. . . ."

I turned to the shelves of books. There were several series of boys' books which looked old. *The Rover Boys* must have belonged to that man in the red tie downstairs, if not to his father before him. My hand moved over the titles. Kipling. Stories of mystery and buried treasure. One whole shelf of paperbacks. Scott's coin book for 1963. A book about shells.

The Gizzard Family. Oh, Matthew, Matthew. . . .

He had told me about the Gizzards in the hospital last summer when he was trying to make me laugh. "Once there was a whole family named Gizzard."

"Never."

"Yes. There was Mister Ezra Gizzard—he was grizzled. And Lizzie, frizzy-headed Lizzie Gizzard. Also, Isidore. But Isidore got dizzy every time they called him Izzy."

"You are too much."

70

I had the book in my hands, now leafing through it.

They discovered entirely by accident
that by changing the place where the accent went,
their name was Gizzárd (to rhyme with swiss chard).
So Lizzie had her hair unfrizzled,
and Ezra shaved—no more was he grizzled. . . .

I turned to the front of this book of nonsense rhymes about the improbable Gizzards. In a bright, authoritative hand there was written, "For my Matthew on his sixth birthday. Lovingly, Mother."

He had told me that she used to read it to him over and over when he was a little boy. I gave a shake to my head and put the book back on the shelf. I couldn't imagine it. Someday I would think all this through and try to figure it out; it was too much for me tonight. I selected one of the paperback mysteries. Maybe later I could read myself to sleep.

Over at the chest I opened a drawer and saw socks, handkerchiefs, a flashlight. In another drawer I found pajamas, as Mrs. Kinsolving had told me I would. They were striped, blue and white; I undressed and put them on, tying the drawstring up over my great bulge in a way that was not entirely satisfactory but would do well enough for one night. I rolled up the arms and legs and went to the closet to look for a robe.

There was one hanging on a hook just inside the door, of dark, patterned silk. I started to put it on and was overwhelmed by what I had thought I had forgotten—the scent of him, spicy like his shaving lotion, male, cigarette-y.

I drew the sleeve across my face. *Oh, Matthew, why did you write your mother about me?* I wiped my eyes on the

71

sleeve and put it back on the hook. Another robe was on a hanger, white terry cloth, laundered since it was last worn. Yes, this would be better for the state I was in tonight. I put it on and rolled up the sleeves and opened the door into the hall.

The wastebasket that had been sitting there had been taken away. It was just as well. It was sure to have held letters, maybe from all the way back to Culver. There might have been a diary full of his sweet, cornball observances about life and pearls. I would have read every line, probably crying my eyes out. And I knew I was not up to any more of an emotional binge than I'd already been on since coming to this house those few hours ago.

At the door I paused to get my bearings, figuring out the layout: The house faced north, and my room was on the north; this wing, just over the bedroom wing downstairs, ran to the west; Mrs. Kinsolving's room was on the south of that wing, and the room where I had glimpsed Kathleen this afternoon was probably just about under mine.

The bathroom was to my right at the end of the hall. It was older than the one downstairs, probably one of the first put in this house. There was a long chain which you pulled, letting loose an unbelievably noisy avalanche. There was a tub of metal, probably copper, with greenish streaks, which was enclosed all around by wood. More of that stained glass at the upper part of the window, dull now with the darkness outside. A lavatory, quite ornate, on a pedestal, had a bowl badly stained with drops from a tap I couldn't tighten. Dust had been swiped in streaks here and there. It was not hard to believe that they never came upstairs.

But there were fresh towels laid out, big ones, thick and white, and small ones of thin, white linen. Hand-embroidered monograms on the linen towels had a big *K* in the middle with an *M* to the left and a *G* to the right. The *M* was for Maria, but I had no idea what the *G* stood for.

Her maiden name would have been something German, I'd have bet on it. Mrs. Kinsolving was my idea of what the ideal Nazi female would be like. My first impression of Mother-of-the-Year had been overlaid with another one now. That Ilse something—was it Koch? Yes; I had studied about her in history last year. The one they called the Bitch of Buchenwald, the one who made lampshades out of human skin.

I looked at my face in the clouded mirror that was so low Matthew must have had to stoop a little to look into it. *Oh, Math, what would you say to me if you were here now? What sweet nugget of wisdom would you produce for my comfort?*

I had another thought: Had he, even my Matthew, not been quite as dear and uncomplicated as I had thought him to be? My face showed the strain of these hours in this house.

I scrubbed my teeth again with a washcloth.

Back in my room, I opened the window a little wider. It was a bit cooler now. I heard the moving river, the whispering of the ivy. Just outside the window was one of the little balconies I had seen this afternoon; it was strictly for ornamentation with not even room enough for a chair.

For a little while I stood there looking across the bay toward the village, where I could see a few lights. If I had come here with Matthew, he would be turning to me about now to say, "Well, darling, what did you think of my mother?" I would have searched for something nice to say —beautiful hair, marvelous teeth. But I had not come with him. If he had brought me here as his bride, I knew

73

that Mrs. Kinsolving would have treated me very differently.

If, if, if. . . .

I turned on the radio. It was ten o'clock, and I set my watch. The news was depressing: the war; a riot; an earthquake somewhere; flooding in the north central part of the state. I turned the dial past a blurred succession of rock and roll sounds, country music. But there was too much static to try to listen to anything, so I turned it off.

There was a reading light over the bed; I adjusted it, put back the plaid bedspread. Under it was a blanket, which it was hard to imagine needing on a close, humid night like this, but I left it in case I should need it in the night. The mattress was firm, the kind Matthew had liked. After I had read the first couple of pages in the mystery, I discovered it was one I had read before.

Steps were coming along the hall, shuffling. I heard a bumping sound at the door. It scared me a little.

"Come in—?"

Nobody came in. That bumping against the door again. And then a voice making garbled sounds. Kathleen.

I opened the door, and she stood there with an aluminum tray and a cup of thick china, which held a dark, steaming liquid that looked like cocoa. It was like boarding school again, I thought; they'd give you hot cocoa to make you sleep no matter if the temperature stood at 102.

Kathleen's eyes darted up and then down at the cocoa, as if she were terrified of spilling it. She had the strangest eyes I'd ever seen, with irises that were like broken, gray glass. This was the first time I'd had a chance to take a good look at the girl who was so unbelievably Matthew's sister.

74

I took the tray from her unsteady hands and set it on the bedside table.

"Kathleen, how nice of you to bother. Thank you." My hand touched her arm, patting it. I had the feeling that it was necessary to soothe her, reassure her.

"Do you know who I am, Kathleen?"

She stared at me blankly from under the tangled hair.

"I am Francesca. I am Matthew's wife. Do you remember Matthew? Your brother Matthew, Kathleen?"

She had the face of a good child, but it was unfinished. There was a looseness to the expression as if it wanted a mind to pull it together. I noticed that her eyes seemed to move all the time as if she had little control over them. Or as if she were perpetually frightened.

There was a torrent now of vowel sounds, almost without consonants, which were punctuated by soblike breaks. I thought, she is upset by something. Over and over, she was repeating the same sound. It sounded almost like . . . kitty?

"Oh," I said, relieved. "The kitty. Yes, the poor kitty, Kathleen. I am sorry. I always wanted a kitty when I was a little girl, but my mother wouldn't . . ." I stopped. Allegra hadn't been my mother; I couldn't remember my mother.

And then I thought of Mrs. Kinsolving and knew there was not always a blessing in having a mother.

The babbling continued, eerily musical, but I couldn't understand one word. I wished she would go now.

"Thank you for coming, Kathleen. It was . . . so nice of you . . . to bring me the cocoa." I spoke distinctly, slowly, hoping she could understand me.

"Eh—eh—" she was bobbing her head, giving me that loose smile.

75

"Good night, now, Kathleen." My hand was on her arm, propelling her gently toward the door, although I felt her reluctance to leave. I was sorry for her, but I was afraid I might not be able to go to sleep if I had to listen to those sounds any longer.

With a sudden, hesitant gesture she put out her hand and touched my face, moving it along my cheek. It was so rough for a young girl's hand, as if she worked very hard. Tears were brimming in the shattered-glass eyes. It was as if she cried because she could not communicate.

I touched the wild, dark hair with pity. "I wish I knew what you were trying to tell me, Kathleen. I am sorry—"

She shook her head, murmured, looking frightened again. And then she turned away.

From the doorway I watched her walk down the carpeted hall in that shapeless, gray uniform. She was young, but there was no spring of youth in that shuffling step. She was childlike, but there was no joy.

What is her IQ? I wondered. Forty—fifty? And what is the name for her terrible problem? She did not look like my idea of a Mongolian. That must have been quite some school they had sent her to—however expensive—if they had not even helped her learn to talk.

I closed my door. It was all too much . . . Mrs. Kinsolving who could not hear . . . Kathleen who could not talk.

The cocoa sent up steam under the light. It was hard to imagine anything less appealing on a sultry night like this, but maybe this was a nurse type of thing to do or Southern hospitality or something. It was dark brown, as if heavy on chocolate. I took one sip and then put it down. It was bitter, very bitter.

My heart began a funny, fluttery pounding. There was

something more than just chocolate in that drink. Maybe Mrs. Kinsolving was trying to kill me.

I carried the cocoa into the bathroom, poured it into the stained washbowl, and washed it away. In the clouded mirror I caught a glimpse of my face.

Francesca, poor thing, you are cracking up. That woman wouldn't kill you. She hates you, true, but not that much. She's not really that Nazi Ilse who was so artsy-craftsy with the lampshades. Poor Mrs. K just has one of those mother-son hang-ups, which is so common it's boring. All she did was open a sleeping capsule—sure, a nurse could get plenty of sleeping capsules—and drop it in the cocoa so you could get a good night's sleep and be ready to leave her house in the morning.

Ready? I rolled my eyes and reached up to turn off the light over the mirror. I could hardly wait to be on my merry way.

Back in my room, for no very sensible reason, I decided to lock my door. But there was no key in the lock. I turned off the light over the bed and tried to sleep to hurry the morning.

As usual, my child moved a lot. Surely these turnings and impatient kicks must mean that he was alert and normal. What if, tomorrow, I just said nothing at all to Miss Gee about what I had learned about the taint in the Kinsolving family? She mentioned forms I would fill out. There would be spaces, I supposed, having to do with hereditary defects. What if I just left those spaces blank, pretending I knew nothing?

No, no. I could never like myself again.

I turned, trying to get the two of us comfortable, making a conscious effort to worry about something else. I thought about Mrs. Kinsolving asking if the child were

Matthew's. That question, I knew, had been thrown in only for sadistic effect; I wasn't going to worry about it.

How different my mother-in-law had been at the dinner table. All gone, that smiling politeness of those minutes in the library when I had felt like an Avon lady. If she had asked me that question then, had hurled those accusations at me there, I would have left at once. It would have been so easy for me to have left while it was still daylight.

It was almost as if she had not wanted to give me any reason then for leaving in anger, had wanted to keep me here for a few hours. Until dark.

Why? Why? What possible reason could that strange woman have had for wanting to keep me in this house until the bus had gone and it was completely dark?

Maybe she had thought I would talk to them at the Red and White Café. To that boy, that poor, nothing boy, and his grandmother, the "character" whom I had not seen. She might have been afraid I would tell them she had been unkind. Even though she scorned the villagers, it was probably true that she prized her image—the *grande dame,* the proud lady of the castle, who drove past like royalty in her big, black Lincoln, but who "waved like anybody else."

This line of reasoning seemed to make sense. Much as I disliked the woman, I had to admit that she had a certain dignity. She would hardly lower herself to the point where she would explain to anybody over there why she had treated me badly. And I was very sure she would never, not even to excuse herself, air dirty linen to the extent that she would tell about the letter Matthew had written about me.

I have kept his letter, she said.

78

I thought: *I would give anything on earth to see that letter.*

Completely wide-awake, I stared at the dim ceiling, not tired at all now. The letter was almost sure to be down there on that cluttered desk in the library. This afternoon I might have found it if I had known enough to look for it when she went to get me that glass of water. Tonight, while I sat down there in the hall all that time waiting for her to ready this room, I would have had plenty of time to have gone through everything in that desk.

And I thought: *I am going to get up and go down there and find it.*

Yes. Get up now. Go. . . .

Chapter 6

AT SCHOOL when the other girls went downstairs in the middle of the night to the dark kitchen to swipe bread or something, they always went without me. In a book when some brainless girl gets up in a dark house to investigate mysterious lights in the old icehouse or noises down in the cellar instead of putting her head sensibly under the covers, I stop reading. Always. In the first place, books like that scare me. In the second place, I can't bring myself to care what happens to girls who are that stupid.

This was different; it was necessary to my peace of mind. I turned on the bed light and reached for the white terry cloth robe I had put across the foot of the bed. I was shaking like the true coward that I was, but I knew I would never forgive myself if I didn't at least try, on my one night in this house, to find that letter Matthew had written to his mother.

How might he have phrased it? "I love Francesca, and I know you will love her, too. She has made a mistake, and we must help her. If you understand how everything happened, I think you will be able to help her more while I am in Vietnam . . ."

Yes, I was sure that Matthew would have said something like that.

My pajama legs had fallen down, and I rolled them up, not wanting to be tripped on those stairs. *What were you doing down here?* (I could just hear that hollow voice.) *Stealing the spoons, Mrs. Kinsolving.* I giggled nervously as I went over to the chest to get some safety pins to secure my pajama legs. I have always had an insane urge to laugh when I am scared.

I stood in the middle of the room, trying to think. I had seen a flashlight . . . but where? Not on the shelves. Not in the desk drawers; they were empty. It was in the small drawer at the top of the chest, the one with the handkerchiefs and socks.

By now the battery might be run-down. I pressed the button. The beam was feeble, but it would be strong enough to let me see where I was going. I turned off the light in my room, though for no particular reason. Her room was on the other side of this wing, and even if she chanced to see my light now at nearly midnight, she would hardly come upstairs to see why the sleeping pill hadn't made me sleep.

From time to time I paused as I made my way along the carpeted passage into the large hall with the leaning portraits. The house was not absolutely quiet. A stiff breeze seemed to have come up and was rattling a shade somewhere. The sound of the refrigerator going on in the kitchen made me pause and snap off my flashlight at the turn of the stairs.

My heart, pounding in my ears, made more noise than anything.

When I reached the big downstairs hall, I could look along the bedroom wing and see that there was no light showing under any of the doors.

I had my flashlight turned off now. Enough moonlight was coming through the windows on the dining room side so that I could make my way. Also, I realized that there was enough light to show me up plainly in this white robe, like an overweight ghost. I would scare the wits out of anybody. Again I had that nervous urge to giggle.

Remembering the loose threads in the Oriental rug, I stepped carefully in the library. The top of the desk had been closed since I had been in here this afternoon, but fortunately it had not been locked. Carefully, I opened it, turned on the flashlight beam. I told myself it should not take long to look through this pile, even though the pile was a big one. All I had to do was to look for a handwritten letter in the bold black of those fiber-tipped pens that Matthew always used.

A typed letter on business stationery lay open on top of the pile. I pushed it to one side, and as I did so, my own name jumped out at me halfway down the typed page.

I can see now the way the flashlight beam jerked back and forth on that letter, going from my name up to the letterhead that said, CAL-STATE INVESTIGATIVE AGENCY in bold letters at the top, to the right to pick up the date which was sometime in October last fall, to my name again where it said, "Re: Francesca Cabbot Kinsolving." There was a signature scrawled at the bottom of the letter, which I didn't take time to decipher.

I gulped my way through that letter, skimming the block paragraphs, which were numbered. The first was biographical, and I skipped that; I knew where I was born and where I had lived. The second had to do with Merriam College and my scholarship and my job for the professor, and I couldn't bother with that either for now.

The yellow circle of light trembled on paragraph three: ". . . gunshot wound by her own hand . . . letter alleging numerous intimacies between husband and subject, then Francesca Cabbot . . . college authorities, investigating, concurred with evidence in letter of deceased and presented by numerous members of the college community . . . subject was dismissed from college in May . . . subsequent cancellation of all scholarship benefits . . ."

Paragraph four: "Subject took up residence in abandoned cottage on beach near Cayce, California . . . septicemia . . . hospitalization . . . applied for license to wed. . . .

There was more. It was all here, all, all, all.

But my Matthew had not told her.

I was trembling. I drew the white robe around me, feeling as if my dear love had his arms close around me. *Oh, Math. Oh, darling. You didn't tell your mother. Forgive me, forgive me, please. I should have had some faith.*

I needed to cry. I could not take time to cry here now, but my eyes were so full of tears I could not see. I wiped them on my sleeve, my mind whirling with questions: Why had that letter been lying here on top of the pile? Had she just been reading it before I came? But that would be an unlikely coincidence since she had not known I was coming.

And yet this afternoon, while I was lying down in her room, she would have had plenty of time to have come here and gotten the letter out and read it again to refresh her memory with the facts. Yes, that was it. I knew.

A movement on the floor caught my eye. I looked down into luminous eyes that were not unlike Mrs. Kinsolving's. My indrawn breath was almost a scream. Oh, cat, don't start crying! She meowed once hoarsely, and I leaned to pet her. She moved away from me, looking back at me distrustfully.

I steadied the flashlight and was about to start reading every word of the letter from the top when I heard a sound.

I turned off the flashlight beam and stood motionless, feeling my hair prickle on my scalp. Slowly I turned and saw a sliver of light showing under the door that led to the kitchen. I heard a sound, as if ice cubes were being loosened. Maybe Mrs. Kinsolving had gone to the kitchen to get herself a drink of cold water.

I breathed raggedly, knowing that to get to the kitchen she must have gone across the back part of the hall from her room while I stood here reading that letter. How had she missed noticing the glimmer of light in this room? What would I have done if she had caught me? I could well imagine the fury in those pale eyes. What should I do now? Wait for her to get that water and go back to bed?

I waited a long minute, and then another thought hit me. What if Mrs. Kinsolving should get to thinking about the letter, remember she had left it on top, and then decide to come in here now and put it in a safer place?

She would turn on the light. I looked around the dark room. There was no place at all for me to hide.

Other sounds came from the kitchen, as if she might have decided on a midnight snack. I closed the desk the way it had been and moved quietly, quickly across the big hall. I agonized over the creaks on the stairs until I remembered my mother-in-law's deafness, and then I hurried the rest of the way past all the portraits, back to Matthew's dark room and his big firm bed.

My heartbeats shook the bed as I lay there. I was trembling with exhaustion, relief. Matthew . . . Matthew . . . his presence seemed to be in the room, so strong, so comforting. I calmed gradually, slept after awhile.

But it was a troubled sleep. I dreamed of Kathleen and her broken eyes, mourning, saying words I could not understand as she held a dead kitten in her hands.

I dreamed of Matthew as I had done every night for such a long time after his death. He held me close, whispering my name, telling me something. But I could not understand his words, either.

The dream moved on. I heard a voice say, "Mother—" It was Matthew. He had come back; he was working on that car out there so it would start in the morning and take me away from this house. I heard a sound, a clatter, as if a wrench might have been thrown down on the cobblestones.

It was so real that I woke up. I sat up, trying to separate dream from reality. Surely I had really heard something out in back of the house. Had my mother-in-law gone out there herself after her midnight snack, remembering some rod, some wire that was not connected? I knew nothing about cars, but I believed I knew her well enough to know she would want to be very sure there would be no further block to my leaving here at the first possible moment.

A crazy picture flashed into my mind of that ivory coiffure bent over the insides of that Lincoln as she knowledgeably rearranged wires and spark plugs, blowing into little things the way men did in garages.

I got out of bed and went to the window to listen. From this room at the front of the house I could not see the courtyard, of course. I could see only the dark bay with a rippled reflection of one light that was shining over at Always. Clouds had covered the moon; there was an uneasiness to the sky, a flickering like lightning, as if a storm might be brewing to the north.

If it's going to rain, I thought, I want to get out of here. I even had the crazy impulse to put on my clothes right then, take the flashlight, and leave the house without a word to Mrs. Kinsolving. But I knew that would be foolish, even dangerous. I stood there for a little while longer, listening, but there were no more sounds out in back.

A telephone rang. A telephone? How could that be when she had said the phone was disconnected? It rang a second time, and then there was silence. I couldn't figure out any possible reason why she would have lied to me about having a phone, but this, at least, was none of my business.

Shivering, although it was not cold, I got back into bed and pulled the thin blanket over me. I almost wished I had drunk that cocoa now, for surely I wouldn't be able to sleep. It must be two o'clock. My mind took up my worries dully. I would tell Miss Gee . . . I would not tell Miss Gee . . . I had to like myself . . . probably the baby would be all right . . . Matthew certainly had been all right . . . Matthew had been perfect.

And he had not, thank God, written that letter to his mother. The thought lulled me. Toward morning I slept heavily.

Someone was shaking my shoulder and calling my name. I opened my eyes and saw Mrs. Kinsolving leaning over me, distraught, her hair down over her shoulders.

"Get up! We must hurry! There has been a cloudburst upstate. The river is rising!"

I sat up. "Will the car—"

"Yes. Get up. Hurry."

"But if there's a flood—"

"We never have floods in June. But hurry, hurry!"

She left. It was barely six o'clock, and the morning was gray. I hurried, my fingers shaking. My clothes on the back of a chair had a damp feeling when I put them on. I saw that it had started to rain a little, and I thought I heard distant thunder.

She was waiting for me at the bottom of the stairs. She said something about the news on the radio. I could hear it going now out in the kitchen. She said a dam had burst and told me where, but the name of the place meant nothing.

With relief I saw that the big, black car sat waiting just outside the door below the terrace steps. She got behind the wheel, and the ancient thing roared to life instantly. She had a heavy foot, Mrs. Kinsolving. We moved ahead with a lurch and roared out of the courtyard and down the drive through the gates.

I could have wept with relief at being underway. Miss Gee behind that big desk would know what to do. I would say . . .

We rounded the curve and saw it ahead of us. The river. It covered the place where the peninsula narrowed. The water was running swiftly, though still not deep.

She gunned the motor as if she would ford the stream or fly over it through the air. We came right to the edge of the water before she stopped the car. I braced myself against the dashboard so I wouldn't hit the windshield.

I said, "How long . . . does it usually? . . ."

She did not hear me. She just sat there as if she might still be debating whether or not to make a dash for it. I was so close to tears that I'd have been willing for her to take the chance. It is possible that a big, heavy car like that would have made it.

In a dull voice she said the same thing she had said before: "We never have floods in June. We must go back to the house and see what the radio says." And then she turned to me waspishly and said, "You can't have that baby here!"

That's when I started laughing. She told me to stop,

87

and I turned away. But the laughter was still inside me, and my shoulders were shaking.

"Stop that instantly!"

Helpless, I looked into her furious face. "You said—" and I was off again in a witless, hysterical seizure. I tried to control myself, but oh, how madly hilarious, her commanding me not to have that baby here!

She put her hand on my arm and said, "There, now . . ." as if I had scared her.

I found a handkerchief and wiped my eyes, recovered. I had scared myself.

She backed the car all the way to the house, zigzagging. She said something about breakfast later, but for now I should go to my room.

I turned to her. "In the night I thought I heard a phone. It rang twice."

"You heard my alarm clock. It went off by mistake, and I had a hard time getting it turned off.

"Oh . . ." It didn't matter. I went on past her up the stairs, planning to cry.

Chapter 7

I BELIEVE I remember every single thing that happened that morning. I didn't cry. For a very long time I sat in a chair pulled up to the window, my arms spread on the cool, damp stone of the wide windowsill, looking out through the leaves of the big tree toward the town of Always. Not that I could see much. Sometimes the rain fell so hard I couldn't even see the choppy waters of what had been the little bay but now was part of the rushing river.

I had plugged in the portable radio and put it on the windowsill beside me. The static was almost constant, but so were the weather bulletins: Five inches of rain had fallen somewhere to the north within the last eight hours . . . a bridge had been washed out at a town whose name I had never heard . . . highways this, this, and that were closed . . . warnings had been issued . . . truck farms near the Ohio had been inundated . . . flooding due to saturation after a week of almost constant rain.

I heard the names of rivers I had not known existed: the Mad; the Scioto; the big and Little Miami; the Rattlesnake. All tributary creeks and rivers were helping make the Ohio rise, and it was rising at the rate of two inches per hour.

But the announcer's cheerful voice said there was no undue cause for alarm. Flood control measures had made it impossible for this area ever to have another major flood. The rain would continue today, but gradual clearing could be expected tomorrow with rapid subsiding of high-water levels.

How rapid? I wondered. One day? One week? And how much time, exactly, did I have before this child would be born?

He was very quiet. I had the thought—idiotic—that as long as I sat very quietly, my self-willed child would not waken and want to be born.

Once I had known a girl who was a Christian Scientist. She tried very hard to convert me. I wished now that I had listened. I wished I had one of those little books she kept reading. Think positive thoughts, Francesca, she used to say to me.

I thought positive thoughts. *I will not . . . I will not have this baby born here.* Or was that a negative thought? *I will wait.* That was more positive. *My baby will wait until it is time for him to be born.*

You have to visualize what you want, my friend had told me. You have to see very clearly each small detail of your heart's desire. My heart's desire was a hospital. Nurses in crisp white uniforms and the cheerful rattling of carts in busy halls. Normal, smiling people. A toothbrush. Someone to talk to.

A robin sat on a nest in the big tree just a few feet from the window. I had sat there quite awhile before I even noticed her. But she was watching me with bright, dark eyes, as if she had not taken her eyes from me ever since I first sat down here.

I saw another robin come, his breast a brighter red, and he had a worm in his mouth. He hopped closer, then away, two or three times, and then as if he thought he had confused me, he fed her the worm and flew off into the rain. It made me feel good for a minute. Bird watching had never interested me much, but it was nice now to have this little bit of nature drama to divert me. There were two of them and only one of me, but I wasn't going to pursue that line of thought. At least I didn't have to sit on a nest with the rain pouring down my neck. That was something.

See, Matthew. I am looking on the bright side. Every cloud has its you-know-what.

Kathleen brought me some breakfast, making those sounds I could not understand. I had her put the tray beside me on the wide windowsill. The coffee was in another of those thick, restaurant cups again. I felt pettish about this cup now. Did that woman think I had been blind last night not to have noticed all that lovely thin china in those dining room cabinets? This cup even had a crack in it.

I believed when I saw her I would tell her not to bother. She could have it all, china, silver, everything. I had grown up with fine china and sterling, and once when Allegra feuded with one of my aunts over a set of Limoges, I had been mystified. *Really, Mrs. Kinsolving, your efforts to fool me with your cracked cups are a bore. Relax.*

The cat came in while I was eating. She looked behind the draperies and made hoarse, calling noises, but not hopefully. I tried to tempt her with a bit of food from the tray, but she moved away, looking back at me with those unfriendly Siamese-blue eyes. How long would she look for those babies? I wondered. Would she stop caring when the milk was absorbed? And was it her own discomfort that caused her to look, rather than grief?

Kathleen came into the room. In her hands were a pair of big, open scissors. She came toward me, whacking them open and shut. Blades flashing she reached for my head.

I drew back . . . was she mad, dangerous as well as feeble-minded? But she placed the scissors against her own streaming hair, touched mine again, and I understood.

"Oh." I looked into the strange eyes. "I understand, Kathleen. You want me to cut your hair short like mine?"

"Eh—eh—" She bobbed her head up and down, looking pleased that I had understood.

I closed the scissors and handed them back to her. "No, I can't do that." I shook my head. "I just can't cut your hair, Kathleen. Your mother might not like it."

I was touched by the look of disappointment. "I'm sorry, Kathleen. Someday I will cut your hair. Someday. . . ."

She left, taking the tray. Poor Kathleen, I thought, and the someday that will never come. And then I thought: when I have left this house, it won't bother me at all to remember Mrs. Kinsolving. But Kathleen . . . oh, how I wished I had never had to know about Kathleen.

I got up, conscious that my back was hurting me from having sat so long in one position. Probably it wasn't good for me to sit still like this without exercise. Oh, how morbidly absorbed I had become in my physical state, I thought, noting each twinge, trying to analyze the reasons for each ache.

I felt depressed again, and now I was perversely determined *not* to look on the bright side. I wished I were that bird out there, sitting with the rain running down her neck, unable to feel deeply, to worry. I was tired of the role of Goody Two Shoes. I intended to take a dim view, wallow in self-pity.

But first I would find myself a toothbrush. A bit of slow, careful exercise might be just what I needed. Every bathroom always has extra toothbrushes lying around.

This one was no exception. I found three used toothbrushes in fairly good shape. I chose the best one; it had natural bristles just like the kind Matthew used to use. I couldn't be sure, of course, who had used it, so I started looking around for something to sterilize it with. It seemed logical that I would be able to find some alcohol. I looked on the many shelves, and there was none.

I could have gone downstairs and asked for alcohol or even boiling water, but I was getting some satisfaction out of solving this problem myself. Mrs. Kinsolving hadn't seen fit to come near me all morning, and I didn't intend to ask any favors. There was a linen closet just at the end of this little hall; I had seen the door ajar last night when I first came upstairs. Bathroom supplies, I knew, were sometimes stored in linen closets.

But I found nothing there except stacks of towels, sheets, and other bedding.

I took a couple of steps into the big central hall, noticing the way the smell of mushrooms had intensified with the rain, as if they might actually be growing somewhere in this damp house.

Another thing I noticed was that the faces in the portraits were not so sober after all. They looked almost friendly. And their eyes—it really was very odd—seemed to follow me as I walked across the hall.

I hesitated, looking at all the closed doors. I have some sense of propriety, some reticence about poking around other people's houses when I am a guest, particularly when I am such an unwelcome one. But rather than ask for help in solving this problem, which any thoughtful hostess would have taken care of before now, I was determined that I should find my own alcohol and sterilize this toothbrush which I had ferretted out by myself—no thanks to her. It seemed likely that there would be at least one other bathroom on this floor.

I crossed the hall, glancing down into the color-splashed gloom. Down there in the kitchen I could hear a radio going, turned up loud.

One might have thought, marooned here together as we were, that Mrs. K would have asked me to come downstairs, listen with her to the radio, perhaps have coffee, and worry together.

By now, mercy me, we might have been best friends! I might have discovered that she didn't make lampshades out of human skin after all! We might have laughed over the precious Gizzard family together. She might have produced pictures. *Now here I am, Francesca—oh, a terrible picture of me—with Matthew on his fifth birthday.* She might even have broken open a bottle of medicinal whiskey with a clever remark about warding off snakebite. . . .

My humor was wearing thin. I started opening doors. One, very large, could have been the master bedroom in the old days or perhaps the guest room for visiting dignitaries with its great, carved walnut bed and chests with marble tops. Everything was very dusty with the look of not having been touched for many months. I just looked in at the doors, not entering. Heavy old furniture depressed me. I wanted that even less than I wanted the china and silver. But I did find a second bathroom and, in the medicine cabinet, a bottle of alcohol. I took it with me and continued my prowl.

One room seemed to be a combination sewing room and storage room. I saw trunks, some grocery cartons that had once held sugar, a sewing machine, a very large cutting table, a dress form with a piece of pattern pinned to it. I noticed a telephone near the sewing machine, as if it had been installed so that the busy seamstress would not have to leave her work to answer the phone when it rang. Why, I wondered, if she was so well set-up for sewing, didn't she get on the ball and make some decent dresses for poor Kathleen?

There was a billiard room off the wing over the kitchen, quite large, with an enormous table covered with green. I saw evidence of mice and had the thought that Mrs. Kinsolving would have done well to let that cat keep her kittens. Another room off this wing seemed to have been Matthew's playroom when he was a little boy. I had no more desire to enter it than any of the others, even though I knew he must have played with the erector set, the trucks, that train with its little tunnels, its dusty village.

It struck me as sad that there were no dolls, no dollhouses, or other little-girl toys. Poor Kathleen. But then she had always been away in that school.

The last door stuck. I tugged, and when it opened, I stood there a bit uneasily. It wasn't a room. Stairs went straight down without turning, apparently to the kitchen. I could hear the radio very clearly down there, could smell something spicy cooking.

Another flight of stairs went up, at a different angle, to the third floor. The sound of the rain was very loud on the roof, accentuating the feeling of the storm. It wasn't an ordinary attic up there; I could see more doors and knew that in the old days those had very likely been the servants' rooms.

Where did all the money go? I wondered. Matthew had said they were far from rich now, but that was just another of those subjects we had never had time to talk about.

My hands were dusty when I finished my tour. I went back to the bathroom I had been using and put the toothbrush to soak in some of the alcohol. When I had washed up, I had a good, long toothbrushing session. Luxury. I was beginning to feel a little better now about everything.

I reached up to pull off the light over the washbowl, and that was when it happened. At first I had no idea what the strange sensation could be. In the mirror I saw my look of shock, surprise. I leaned against the washbowl, holding to the sides. And then I saw the stain, faintly pink, spreading on the white tile of the bathroom floor.

I whimpered, "No, no. . . ."

Back then into Matthew's room, taking short, creeping steps like an old woman. I thought: *Maybe it isn't true. Maybe it doesn't mean anything. Maybe if I lie on the bed, very still, not moving. . . .* I lay down on Matthew's firm bed and pressed my wedding band hard against my lips. I said in that whimpering voice that didn't sound like mine, "Don't get born. Please . . . please. . . ."

I bit my nails and tried to remember that book. "The star, your baby. . . ."

Wait. There had been something about pains. Yes, yes. Everybody had pains. *First,* before anything else. I felt an enormous relief. You had your labor pains first, and you timed them. That was when you were supposed to call your doctor. And then you took your bag which was all packed and ready—the book had been very explicit about what to put in your bag—and you went to the hospital. Just as I would do when the time came.

I had not had pains. There had been only that dull ache in my back. I still had it, but I had noticed that same ache before, and I knew it was nothing. I thought positive thoughts. I visualized the hospital, smelled that hospital smell, heard the cheerful rattling of carts in the corridors. I heard the swish of starched uniforms, the whisper of rubber-soled shoes. I saw friendly, smiling faces all around me.

Last night why hadn't I left this house? Sneaked out that time I woke? Why hadn't I walked, crawled up that hill to the café, screaming for somebody, anybody?

The pain in my back moved around to the front. A dull ache . . . nothing . . . nothing. The hospital would be warm and bright. The hands would be so gentle. I would have somebody call Miss Gee. She had said to let her know if. . . .

A bumping at the door. My lunch on a tray. I pushed my fingers back through my damp hair, not getting up. "Kathleen . . . go get her. Your mother. . . ."

She came almost at once. Her mouth twisted as she looked down at me. Over her shoulder she said sharply to Kathleen who was hovering in the doorway, "Take this tray back down to the kitchen." And then she turned back to me.

That must have been around one o'clock. The dull ache localized, settling quickly into pains that could be timed at about six minutes apart. She gave me a hypodermic. She had not lied about being a nurse. They are not all ministering angels. She jammed that needle home with all the sadistic fervor of every patient-hating, bad nurse in the world.

Midafternoon, maybe later. Another hypo. It was slow to take effect. Above the sounds of the wind and rain, above the sounds I tried not to make, there was another. A heavy knocking against the front door.

She didn't hear it. I roused myself, half sat. "Somebody . . . somebody is out there in front. . . ."

There was a voice calling her name now. A man's voice. She went over to the window and looked out. "Yes?"

I heard a voice shout, "Is everybody all right out here, Mrs. Kinsolving?"

"Yes. Yes, we're all right.'

"Need anything?"

"No. Not a thing."

I sat up, pushed back my sweat-plastered hair. I started trying to get out of bed, clinging to the foot of it. I could hear another voice down there now. It sounded like Red's. "Mrs. Kinsolving, that girl who came out here yesterday—"

Mrs. Kinsolving said in her loud, flat voice, "She has gone. I drove her back to the motel last night. My daughter and I are the only ones here."

I was on my feet, swaying. I cried out, "No, no!" I staggered toward the window, glimpsed Red in a yellow slicker and another man walking down across the lawn to the little dock and the rushing river. I screamed, "Red—Red!"

She slammed the window down and pushed me back.

I fell back on the bed, crying. In a minute I could hear the sound of a motorboat leaving. The boat that could have brought help, a doctor.

I remember dimly the way I screamed at her, blaming her for the pain. Part of the time she was not in the room. Sometime, although I have no idea how long it was after that, she swabbed my arm and gave me another hypo.

And then when I was very far away from this house, from everything . . . maybe a long time later, maybe not long at all . . . she was slapping me on the cheek and calling my name. "Francesca!"

"Don't . . . no."

"Francesca, wake up! You have to help me—you have to cooperate—wake up!"

"Help . . . you. I can't. . . ."

"You must!" She put her face close to mine. "You will die if you just lie there like that!"

Die? . . . Good . . . my mother died when I was born. . . .

Her hands stung my cheeks again.

I tried to do what she said. I took hold of the posts at the head of the bed the way she told me to. My hands were slick with sweat. I did not care about helping.

And then I began to care, for the pain was making itself known to me. Now I was like those bubbles in that bottle, trying to get to the top, desperate for release.

An hour. Maybe two. I reached the top and was released in a fog of nothing . . . nothing.

And through that fog of nothing I heard her say to Kathleen, "Bury it."

Chapter 8

IT WAS the next morning before I really regained consciousness. My mother-in-law had given me too many sedative shots, or they had been too strong, or something. I remember lifting heavy lids from time to time to see that there was a kerosene lamp burning on the big desk and to hear the rain, a continuing, monotonous sound that muted all others.

And every time I surfaced I knew one thing: the baby died. It was better to let myself slip back.

I had come to this house on a Tuesday afternoon. The baby had been born sometime Wednesday evening. It was Thursday morning when I looked at the dullness outside the window and saw that the rain had not stopped as that announcer had promised. The closed panes were rippled with it, and from time to time they rattled with gusts of wind.

On that morning I remember being aware that somewhere along the way I had lost control; an apathy, a grayness had edged my identity aside, and what was left now was not me but an object to which things happened, for which things were done. A binder of some sort had been pinned tightly around my breasts; they hurt a little. Clean pajamas of that same blue-and-white stripe had been placed on me.

My hands moved down over my flatness. Did he die . . . really *die?* How very odd . . . that he should have died. He had seemed so impatient for living. He had such a will of his own. When I leaned too heavily against him, he kicked me. I thought my baby could not wait to be born.

I turned in the bed, stretched my legs. My body was all my own again, without encumbrance. There should be a feeling of relief, not just this sluggishness, this emptiness.

I thought: I am sorry the baby died. It would be more normal, I could like myself better, if I could cry about it. But I pushed that thought away. There was another thought I pushed away: Kathleen out there in the rain. I knew the full impact of those two words I had heard Mrs. Kinsolving say would have to be coped with later.

Footsteps sounded in the hall. I put my arm over my eyes, not wanting to have to talk to anybody just now. Mrs. Kinsolving came into the room with Kathleen. I heard a tray being placed on the bedside table. I smelled coffee.

The sheet was drawn back. I could feel hands moving over me. Do this, she said to Kathleen; do that. She changed the sheet then with careless skill, rolling me like a log from one side of the bed to the other, the way they had done last summer in the hospital in California. She snapped the bottom sheet tight over my feet, and I kicked, trying to free them.

"I know you're awake."

I looked up into the pale eyes. "Is this Thursday?"

"Yes."

"What time is it?"

She glanced at her watch. "It's a quarter past nine."

I set my watch, finding it a little hard to focus my eyes.

And then I forced myself to look at her again, to ask another question. "Why did it die?"

"There is a medical term you wouldn't remember if I told you. She just didn't breathe."

"She—she?" My eyes flew wide. "The baby was a girl? Are you sure?"

She put back her head and closed her eyes as if she might be counting to ten. And then she rolled up the bundle of sheets and handed them to Kathleen.

I got up on one elbow. "I want to know what happened —to—to—the—"

She turned away, pretending she had not heard me. I caught hold of her dress and made her look at me. "There has to be a death certificate. I happen to know that much—" My voice got shrill. "A person can't just bury—"

"She was buried decently in the family cemetery. You will have to take my word for it."

"But it's against the law—"

"Listen—" She flung her arm wide toward the window. "Two people have died over there in just that one little town. It will be days—maybe four or five—before the water goes down. So don't talk to me like a fool of coroners, ministers, priests—"

"But—"

"You didn't want this child. You were going to give it away. I have not forgotten that little detail, even if you have, my girl. So spare me your dramatics. I have enough problems. We have no electricity, and that means no water for you to bathe with. Every single drop that is used up here in the bathroom must be carried up over the stairs. I shall send Kathleen up later with a pan of water so you can take a bath. My knees hurt. I shall hope not to have to come back up over these stairs again today."

In my brain, a bell, a flash of light. Dizzying. My face

must have shown it. I sat up, feeling almost strong and looked up into the big face. "Mrs. Kinsolving?"

Her eyes were like ice on a winter pond. "What now?"

"Do you remember the Gizzards?"

"Are you rational?"

"There was Lizzie Gizzard. Also Ezra and Izzy. . . ."

She turned and left the room.

I swung my feet over the edge of the bed and drew the bedside table with the tray toward me. There was coffee in a thick mug. Orange juice in a cheese glass. Two poached eggs stared up at me with filmed, blinded eyes from a plate that was crazed with heat marks. The tray was dented, a painted, kitchen tray.

My fingers hovered, touching the roughness of the tray as if I were reading Braille. I was thinking of one of my roommates at Merriam College, Jeannie, who walked out of a twenty-fourth-story window after taking LSD. Jeannie was a shy girl, markedly insecure, but she had told me with shining eyes how much of a difference LSD had made in her life when she had first started taking it. "You look at everything with new eyes. Each tiny thing—a dust mote, a grain of sand—has a meaning which must be learned. And if you look at something long enough, you will know everything there is to know."

That's how I felt now, as if everything, each tiny detail, must be examined in the light of the mind-expanding flash that I had just had. I must look, taste, feel, listen as if my life depended on it. And maybe it did.

This woman was not Matthew's mother. If I had not been so involved in my own miseries, I would have known it before now.

That child, that little girl, had not been her grandchild.

She had lied to those men with the boat when they might have brought help that could have saved her.

She did not intend for anyone to know I was in this house. I remembered that she had made a point of saying to the men, "My daughter and I are here alone."

Who was Kathleen? I did not know, but I did not think she was Matthew's sister. Perhaps she was this woman's child. Or a servant. She treated her like one.

Who was this woman? The night I read that letter downstairs I had started in the middle when my own name jumped out at me. But if there had been time for me to read it straight through, the heading might have told me who she was.

How had she taken over this house? And what had happened to Matthew's mother? Had this woman killed her? Had that been a phone I heard ringing in the night? There were so many questions for which I had no answers. I had a feeling that I would not be safe in this house if I betrayed any suspicion.

I was not hungry in spite of not having eaten since yesterday morning, but I forced myself to eat all of the food on the tray, knowing I must try to get back my strength quickly.

The effort of eating tired me. I lay back. *Who is she, Matthew? Come back. Help me.*

There are those who believe that the dead can return. I never have. I didn't know whether Matthew had believed that or not. Very likely not, but then I knew so little about him and his beliefs. Sometimes he went to church, very proper and Episcopalian. We had gone once to a very old native church in Mexico. But the incense put us off. The intensity of belief we saw on the ancient faces made us uneasy. Our colleges had taught us too much.

The professor had believed in reincarnation. (It seems that it's quite acceptable in upper academic circles now to believe in anything that's far out enough.) He had lived many times before, so he told me. Once in ancient Crete and once in India—or had it been Persia? It had been sort of hard for me to follow some of the things he tried to get me interested in. He used to read to me from some sort of Hindu love manual, called the *Kama Satra* or *Sutra* or something like that, which bored me mightily. I had stifled many a yawn. I mean, I didn't need all that weird stuff about the calendar of love and fingernails pressing and phases of the moon. Matthew and I hadn't ever needed it. Had we, darling? Oh, Matthew, come back if you can. I need you.

It was no good. I guess you have to believe in it. I got up, conscious of the aching fullness of my breasts, and found the white robe in the closet. I knew that whatever I did in this house I would have to do alone.

In the mirror I looked at my face. I didn't look ill. Women in primitive cultures, so I had read, delivered their babies in the fields, rested an hour, picked up their hoes, and went on with their work. The birth of my child, I believed, had been a fairly quick and easy one. That woman, whoever she was, was a nurse. For all her roughness and unkindness, she had seemed automatically to do the things that nurses are trained to do. She despised me, but she had not killed me. That, I supposed was something. I tried without much success to be glad about it.

I turned away from the face reflected in the mirror, not liking it.

Matthew . . . did you know our baby died? And did you know about me, all those months I carried her, lacking in the feelings that are instinctive and normal and good? I, too, in my own terrible way, am dead. Something is wrong with me. Allegra used to tell me that. Something is missing, left out. . . .

I sat at the closed window, cold, though wrapped in

Matthew's white robe. The rain fell in blown gray sheets, blocking my view of the opposite shore. The mother robin still huddled on her nest, but the branches of the tree waved like arms in the wind. The look of things had changed in the twenty-four hours since I looked out this window. I could not see the little dock; either it was underwater or had been swept away by the river. The water came halfway up on the lawn now, and some of the trees and shrubbery were half submerged.

If this deluge continued, was it possible that this house could be swept away? I visualized the great gray stones tumbling down the river with the antiques, the silver, the portraits, but I could not bring myself to worry about it. This house had stood for over a hundred years, and it must have survived floods that had been much worse than this.

A movement on the sodden ground near the house caught my eye. Gray shapes moved, darting and sinister. The rats had come, flooded out of their dark places underground. I am a fool over one small mouse, and the thought of a rat almost put me in panic.

A shot. It seemed to come from the side of the house. Somebody was shooting the rats. Another shot, and another. I saw a rat leap into the air, lie still. I pressed my cheek against the window, trying to look in the direction from which the shots seemed to come. I tried to imagine those moonstone eyes sighting along a gun barrel, and I could, well enough. But it didn't seem reasonable to think she would be out there shooting them for the sport of it. Was it necessary, I wondered, to shoot them to keep them from coming into the house?

My apathy was gone now. I got up; I could not bear this anymore, just sitting here fearfully, knowing nothing of what to expect. When was I going to be able to get out of here? I leaned and turned on the radio. Silence. Naturally. Only a battery radio would run without electricity. Maybe she had one downstairs. I had to have some news, had to know what they were saying about the flood.

Odd, how big my sandals were now when I put them on. They were hard to keep on my feet as I crossed the room and made my way along the hall. But these floors up here were too dusty to go barefoot.

I stood in the big upper hall at the head of the stairs, listening. A radio was going down there in the kitchen. I could go down there perfectly well, I was sure, if I took it slowly. I could hold onto the banister, rest there for a minute on the bench at the landing.

I reached the bench and was glad enough to sit down. From here I could see that an old rug had been rolled up and placed before the big front door; little trickles seeped underneath it. A little of the drawing room was visible with its white-shrouded furniture on the left, a little of the dining room on the right. I could not see the portraits of the man in the red tie and the gentle-faced girl beside him. I wished I could. When I got down into the hall, I resolved to take a good look, for I believed now that she was Matthew's mother, Maria. I thought I could remember a similarity in the lift of the dark brows. I wondered again if this woman had killed her.

It was then that I heard voices in the kitchen. I could not distinguish words, but one of them was a man's voice. Red . . . my heart leaped . . . maybe Red had come back!

I stood up and called loudly over the banister, "Mrs. Kinsolving—Mrs. Kinsolving!" This time if Red had come—or whoever—I intended to make sure he knew I was here.

At once she came hurrying through the narrow hall

that led from the kitchen. "What are you doing out of bed?"

I clutched the robe around me. "I heard—I heard a man's voice."

"You heard only the radio. I keep a little battery radio down here in the kitchen."

"Oh." My disappointment was so great I could have cried.

"Now you get back up those stairs to that bed. You're old enough to have sense enough to take care of yourself."

I was trembling when I made my way back up the stairs, but more from the dashing of my sudden hope than anything else. Almost as soon as I was on the bed pulling the sheet up over me, she was walking into the room with a hypodermic syringe in her hand.

"I don't need anything—I don't want anything. Really, I feel perfectly well, perfectly strong—"

"Nonsense. Roll up your sleeve. I should have given this to you this morning. I just forgot it. It is always necessary for girls to sleep a great deal after childbirth."

I didn't believe it. I covered my arm. "No, please—"

She was strong and practiced, and I was weak. The needle went deep, hurting.

I lay still when she had gone, frightened. I knew I must think fast before the shot took effect. She didn't want me up prowling around. Could that possibly have been a man's voice I heard in the kitchen?

No, no, it must have been only the radio. Nobody would be coming out here now. Nobody knew nor cared that I was here.

And then, with my mind beginning to dull, I had a thought that frightened me more than any of the others: She must be, after all, Mrs. Kinsolving. That man who had come in the boat with Red had called her by name. And the boy at the café had said something about "all that white hair."

It was better to give myself to oblivion. Too much fear waited on the next plateau.

Toward evening I roused again. My breasts hurt quite a bit now. That kerosene lamp was burning, and she was in the room. In her hands she held a large glass of yellowish liquid.

"Here is an eggnog for you. Two eggs in it. You must get back your strength."

My mind had no sharpness. My lips were very dry, and I drank most of the eggnog thirstily before I lay back. The front of my pajamas was wet. I pressed my hands against the swelling ache and said, "I should have . . ."—it was hard to form the words—"I should have . . . seen her. You should have let me see my little girl. . . ."

She said shortly, "You should thank me. Have you ever seen one of them?"

"*Them?*"

"You gave birth to a monster."

I cried out.

There were vertical lines around her tightened lips. "As I told you, that is the medical term for a severely deformed child. Put it out of your mind. You should be glad you did not have to look at it. When you leave here, you can forget it. Just forget this whole thing. Forget that any of this ever happened."

She had another hypo for me. I did not protest. I wanted to forget.

I slept without dreams. When I awoke I was in a nightmare. Black dark was in that room, hands were on me. I screamed, and a hand covered my mouth. I fought the hand away.

Low babbled sounds in that other language. Kathleen.

"Bay-ay—" she seemed to be saying. "Bay—" There was an urgency in the voice, the hands.

"The bay?" I tried to see her face in the dark room. Oh, the bay outside. The water must have risen. The house must be in danger. Kathleen was my friend.

Confused, I let her get me out of bed. I reached for my robe, dragging it around my shoulders. She helped me as I was trying to get my sandals on my feet. She had a flashlight with a bright beam. She kept murmuring as she guided me along the corridor.

We were in the big hall now, and I moved toward the stairs, but she restrained me. I turned and saw in the dimness that she had her fingers to her lips. She made that sound like, "Kitty—" but it made no sense. None of this was making any sense.

Dazed, I let her guide me across the big hall. She was tugging at a door that stuck. Now I could see that this was the door that opened onto the stairs leading down to the kitchen. I started to go down, but she was urging me upward.

The beat of the rain was louder here. I tried to hang onto reality. Had the water risen so high that we must get to the top of the house or be drowned? Would we cling then to the rooftop in hope of rescue? She was trying to hold the flashlight so that I could see the stairs, but I kept stumbling. Oh, God, I thought, I don't want to die like this, my mind blurred, not able to think clearly nor to do anything to help myself.

We were in the third-floor hall. We moved past some closed doors to other stairs. The tower. The cat was up there. I could hear it crying.

I had forgotten about the tower. Up those stairs, very steep and narrow, to another door with light showing under it. It was closed, but I could hear the cat plainly in there now, crying.

No, not a cat.

A red, naked baby lay on a cot, screaming. Flailing arms and legs had kicked aside a blanket she had been wrapped in. I fell on my knees beside her. My frantic hands went over her perfect body. She lay in wetness.

I drew her and the sopping blanket into my arms. Kathleen's clumsy hands were fumbling at the buttons on the front of my pajamas. She helped me loosen the binder.

"Girl—" I said, "hush . . . hush. . . ." I was crying so that I could hardly see.

She tried to suck and then cried at me angrily. She sucked again. Cried. And then settled to learning.

It hurt me. And then, in an agony of relief, it didn't hurt at all.

I rocked back and forth on the floor as I held her in my arms. I touched the perfection of her, the mop of thick, black hair. I whispered, "I know you . . . I know you." She had made herself known to me long weeks ago, impatient, strong-willed. I should have known she would not die so easily.

Kathleen's loose face was radiant in the soft glow of the kerosene lamp which sat on the floor. "Bay-ay—" She put out her rough hand to caress. "Bay. . . ."

Chapter 9

CRAMPED, I got up and moved with my sleeping child to the sagging cot. My knees trembled, my arms felt weak, but I was not ready to put her down.

How? Why?

I still felt dazed, not sure that any of this could be anything but one of my vivid dreams. And yet, my senses were functioning in an undreamlike way. There was a smell to the baby that was far removed from any of Allegra's pink, powdered infants. All of her babies had been bald at birth, but this child's hair was inches long, almost black, like the hair on some funny little doll. And there was the lightly breathing, warm, living weight of her in my arms that never had been a part of any of my dreams.

The chimney on the kerosene lamp was so blackened that there was only the most shadowy illumination. Windows on all four sides of this little room were small and narrow, as in a castle. The construction here was of heavy wooden beams and stone. On one of the wooden sills I saw a glass of milk with a spoon in it, and I knew that Kathleen must have made some attempt to feed the baby when she started screaming.

When had that been? Had all the narcotics injected into my veins before her birth made her, too, lose many hours?

Might that be the reason she had seemed to be lifeless at birth?

I looked at Kathleen's simple, blissful face and knew I would never know the answers to all my questions.

I smiled at her as I rocked a little back and forth. "I didn't know what you were saying, Kathleen. I thought you were trying to tell me the bay had risen. And then when I heard her, I thought it was the cat who was crying. I thought you had been saying, "Kitty . . . kitty—""

The girl's face underwent a change. Her eyes widened fearfully. She caught hold of my arm and again said those syllables that sounded like "kitty." Her face was distorted in her frustration at trying to make me understand.

"Never mind, Kathleen. It doesn't matter."

She opened her mouth and said with great effort, "Keh-hee. Keh-hee—"

I knew she had trouble with consonants. She had said, "Bay-ay for baby. What consonant was missing here?

"Kibby? Kicky? Kiddy?—" I went down the alphabet. I stopped. A chill moved over me. "Kenny?"

"Eh-eh." She nodded, rocked with agitation, her shattered eyes darting.

Kenny. Matthew's cousin. The cruel one who stole his ring and took the shell off the turtle. I held the baby close. I knew now who the woman was. The men in the boat had called her Mrs. Kinsolving because she *was* Mrs. Kinsolving. She was Kenny Kinsolving's mother. I knew now whose voice I had heard in the kitchen. I knew who had been shooting the rats.

"Kenny is . . . is he your brother?"

"Eh—eh." Kathleen rolled up her sleeve and showed me bruises that looked like the marks of fingers.

My mind was going off in several directions, all frightening, many with question marks. I tried to concentrate on what I thought must be the truth, or close to the truth:

Mrs. Kinsolving thought the baby was dead when she didn't breathe at birth. She was—I still held to this thought—not a murderer, but on the other hand she was not one to try to revive the blood heir to this place which she intended to keep for her own.

Kathleen had been sent out there in the night with those awful words which had penetrated my stupor: Bury it. Kathleen, tenderhearted, needing so badly to have something to love, to mother. The kittens had been drowned. Even that last one she had hidden was searched out and destroyed.

I looked down at the small, lovely face. Some miracle of night air, the rain, rough handling . . . something . . . had revived her. I could imagine Kathleen's joy when she found the baby lived and then the fear that must have seeped into the slow mind. And so she had hidden her here and done what she could to keep her alive.

I wondered again when hunger had roused the baby to cry the way I had heard her crying? That was another thing I would never know. If Kathleen had not come to get me when she did, it was possible that Kenny, whose hearing was presumably normal, might have heard her. And yet with the noise of the storm and that radio going down there all the time three floors below. . . .

"Is Kenny in this house now?"

"Eh—eh—" She nodded.

"Where is he sleeping?"

She pointed downward vaguely.

"Near your room?"

She nodded again.

I moaned, "Oh, Kathleen, what are we going to do?"

She made those incoherent noises. I knew she couldn't help me. She had done awfully well to manage thus far.

My eyes searched the room. There was only this sagging, narrow cot, a chair, an old trunk, a chest, and a broken mirror sitting on the floor. I would stay here, not go back to my room. In the morning Mrs. Kinsolving would come to my room and find it empty. She might think that I had tried to get away, had drowned. And then when the water went down, I would carry this baby, escape from this house. . . .

No, no. Four days, she had said, maybe five before the water would go down. It wasn't sensible to think that we could live up here that long without detection. There would be only this poor, benighted girl to help us survive. She hadn't the craftiness necessary to keep such a secret for that long.

All right. I would take the baby back to my room right now. When Mrs. Kinsolving came in the morning, I would let her see that the child lived. I said to myself the words I had said before: She is not a murderer.

But Kenny. What did I know about him? He was cruel. Obviously he was hiding here for some reason I could not guess. His mother had told the men, "Only my daughter and I are here."

Had he been here when I first came? I thought so. It could have been Kenny whom I heard that first night getting ice cubes in the kitchen when I found the letter in the library. He might have been the one who worked on the car in the night. He could have been the one who heard the news of the flood so early in the morning, roused his mother, and told her to get me out of here.

One fact emerged clearly: Neither Kenny nor his mother wanted me to know he was here. That was why she had knocked me out again today. That was why she was feeding me so well, trying to get me on my feet so that, at the first possible moment, I could get out of here. She had added her own fiendish lie to ensure making my memory of all this so terrible that I would never want to come back. Put it out of your mind, she had said. Forget all about what happened here.

I put the baby down on the cot and then took the white bathrobe from my shoulders and folded it around her. As a diaper, a blanket, a nest. How long would she sleep before she roused and cried again? Three hours? I looked at my watch and saw that it was just past three thirty.

"We must go downstairs now, Kathleen. Downstairs. We must try not to make any noise."

"Bay-ay?"

"The baby will be all right. We must not . . . we must not let anybody . . . not anybody . . . find out she is here."

"Eh—eh."

My arms drew her close. "Oh, Kathleen, help me, help me. I don't have anybody else to help me but you." I looked into the strange, half-comprehending eyes, wishing I knew just how much the poor creature could understand.

"You must go back to your bed now. Walk on tiptoe. Be very quiet." I put my finger to my lips. She did the same and said, "Sh-h, sh-h," as if pleased to have understood. And then, "Bay-ay?"

"Don't worry. The baby will be all right . . . all right, Kathleen. I will feed her again before she cries. Please don't . . . you *must not* . . . come up here again." I knew that was asking an awful lot of a girl whose intelligence was so limited, but she seemed to understand.

I leaned over my daughter. She slept with fists curled tight on either side of her beautifully shaped head. It frightened me to leave her here, but I was afraid to do anything else.

I blew out the kerosene lamp and closed the door of

the tower room. Together, Kathleen and I went down the stairs to the third floor, the second. In the big upper hall I stood holding my breath at the head of the stairs while she continued on down. She was so clumsy; even barefoot that girl made a noise. Mrs. Kinsolving would not hear her, but Kenny might. I waited for her to knock over a chair, bump into a door, but she made it into her room with only a final, frightened pound of heavy steps.

Back in my room I didn't want to sleep, didn't dare. I got that other robe from the closet, the dark one of patterned silk which I hadn't felt I could wear that first night. I needed now more than ever to feel that there was something of Matthew left in this house to help me.

No. I didn't believe in that. I was on my own.

I walked up and down, going from almost unbearable joy to a frenzy that seemed to paralyze my brain. I ran my fingers through my hair, pulling, as if I could drag out some thought, some sensible plan. *God, if I have any intelligence, let me use it now.* But my mind was a blank. I knew this house was a trap from which we might not escape alive.

I sat at the desk, lit the lamp. I wished I had some paper so I could write everything down and see it more clearly.

How about the truth, the whole truth, in an appeal to Mrs. Kinsolving? *Mrs. Kinsolving, I know who you are, and I know this house and everything in it is probably mine. You have no right to be here. But you can have the house. I will sign anything you want me to sign. . . .* No, no. That was too stupid an idea to finish.

I would do better to keep my mouth shut, play it stupid. That was her opinion of me, obviously enough.

And God knows I had been stupid! Hadn't I believed, that first afternoon, her story about why she had not written me? All that malarkey about how she had been crushed, destroyed, because Matthew had not spent his last leave with her. Hadn't I believed her when she told me that Matthew had written her all those things about what happened at Merriam College? Yes. That was really stupid. I should have known Math better than that.

When she told me that cruel lie about the baby, I had accepted that for truth also. No doubt, to some extent, she had played it by ear, and this must have seemed a fine touch, a bit of extra insurance that this would be such a horrible experience I would want to put it out of my memory as soon as possible.

I went further back, all the way to the beginning of Matthew and me. He had written his mother about us in late July or early August. Maria Kinsolving had replied at once with that letter I had not seen, and that was the last time he had heard from her. This Mrs. Kinsolving had made no mention of that letter, probably because she never had known about it. She had mentioned her illness. But what if it was Matthew's mother who had been the one who was ill along about then? And what if this Mrs. Kinsolving had come here then as a nurse to take care of her?

Yes, yes. As I sat there in the early hours with the pool of yellow light on Matthew's big desk, I felt that I had cleared a small island of truth in the confusion and lies. I could not be sure when Matthew's mother had died, but for the time being I would assume she had died sometime in late summer. As the nurse and relative living here then, what could have been more natural than for this woman to say she would take care of notifying Matthew of his mother's death?

This, of course, she had never done. At that time she may only have wanted to stay on in this house for a little while. Matthew couldn't have liked her; she might have known he wouldn't let her live here.

At the time of his death I had sent those telegrams here. I wrote that very long letter. Probably that was when she investigated to see how much of a threat I posed.

My letter in November, telling about the baby, must have come as a real blow. Why hadn't she, then or earlier, written me a letter telling me she wanted to have nothing to do with me? I thought about that for a while. Maybe she was afraid I might know Maria Kinsolving's handwriting, might even have in my possession letters which had been written to Matthew. And so she had decided . . . this seemed logical . . . to let sleeping dogs lie. Something in one of my letters may have let her know that I was not very aggressive, and that if she did not acknowledge me, there was a good chance I would not bother her anymore.

And that was almost what had happened. I remembered how I had dreaded coming. I remembered how, on the day I did come, my courage kept ebbing, how I even hoped, finally, that no one would answer the door.

How dismayed she must have been when she saw me. She had stood there without a word at first. Maybe she had been debating whether or not she dared let me walk away. I remembered the way she had questioned me about the "tiresome old man" who drove the bus—had I talked to him? To the old woman who ran the café? No, no. I had not talked to either one of them. I had let her know I knew nothing.

What a sigh of relief she must have drawn. From there on it had seemed simple. Keep me here for dinner. Let me have it then between the eyes. And if her shrewd guess of my character was right, that would finish me off for good.

And it would have. Francesca, the Gutless Wonder, would have been so easily finished off then, wanting only to leave this house and never look back.

If her car had started. *But* her car would not start.

That if and that but had marooned me here. I sat now at this desk with my knuckles pressed against my teeth. I had not smoked for months, but I wished I had a cigarette now . . . a pack . . . a carton. . . .

Upstairs a baby girl was sleeping. Downstairs they were sleeping. I, here in the middle, was awake, knowing more than anyone dreamed I knew. Aware of danger. Aware of responsibility such as I had never had before. I had never been brave, and I was not brave now. I knew only that I was not to be finished off so easily.

Four more days, maybe longer, in this house. Could I keep the baby a secret for that long? And at the end of that time, what then? My brain was too exhausted to try to make a plan.

With relief I turned to the few simple things I must do now, the sort of things any mother would do for her baby. I must get something to clean her off with when she woke up. I remembered having seen a bottle of mineral oil in my forage through the bathrooms. Soft towels would do for diapers; there were safety pins in that drawer over there.

I found the mineral oil readily enough, and I gathered up some soft blankets and towels from the linen closet. The pillowcases would do for nightgowns, after a fashion, if I could cut the corners off the closed end and make a hole for her head to slip through. My resourcefulness pleased me. I wished I knew what had happened to the scissors Kathleen had brought to my room, but she, or someone, had taken them away. Probably I could find some in the sewing room.

I gathered everything up into one of the pillowcases and

turned off my flashlight before I tiptoed across the upper hall to the sewing room. Now that I knew Kenny was in the house, I would take no chances on anything so eye-catching as a flashlight beam.

The windows here were faintly gray now with dawn, but I could not see much. I groped on the big cutting table; it felt gritty with dust. Obviously there was not very much sewing done in this house anymore. I felt along the top of the sewing machine without any luck, but in one of the drawers I found a pair of pinking shears. They would be even better for my purpose.

As I turned to put this last bit of loot into my pillow-case, my hand knocked against the phone, dislodging it from its cradle. Automatically, I replaced it, remembering that time I had thought I heard a phone ring. What if—? I snatched it up and listened. And then I put it back. Nothing in this house was going to be that easy for me. This phone was as dead as if the wires had been cut.

The face of my watch was just barely visible; it was almost five. I crossed the hall and very carefully opened the door that stuck. I listened, but there was only silence down in the kitchen. My heart swelling with excitement, thankfulness, I went up the stairs.

The faint light in the tower room showed me that the baby lay exactly as I had left her, still wrapped in Matthew's robe as if she had not moved. It scared me. I leaned over her to assure myself that she still breathed. There were some matches beside the lamp, and I lighted it and placed it so that it cast a halo of light around her. For a while I just knelt there, worshiping this small, not very clean girl.

I touched the tiny, closed fist. "Maria," I whispered. "Maria. . . ."

Her eyelids quivered but did not open. With what ease

I had slid into this most hackneyed groove of all—the adoring mother who is stunned by her firstborn's perfection. Look at those lashes—most babies didn't even have lashes, did they? Look at those fingernails—they needed cutting! Surely this was most unusual. And that hair—I could almost make a little bun on the top and tie it with a ribbon. I longed to show her to someone. *Look, Miss Gee, have you ever?—Now, be frank. . . .*

With the mineral oil I cleaned her, fearing the thin, old linen might be too rough for the new, delicate skin. She woke, trembled, although it did not seem cold to me up there. Hurriedly, I cut the holes to make her pillowcase nightgown. I slipped it over her head and took her into my arms. She nursed, an expert now.

I gloried in my purely animal adequacy. Whatever she needed, I would do for her. I felt strong, almost fierce. I would protect her. With my life? O foolish question!

With awe I thought: I am normal. And I thought: I feel just like Allegra. She used to repeat—disgusting to me then—her doctor's compliments about her splendid milk supply.

My baby was awake when I put her down, but her lashes drifted downward sleepily, enchantingly from time to time. I knew so little about babies. The "good" ones slept most of the time at first, I believed, and I hoped she was one of those. If she should cry, the noise of the wind and rain ought to be enough to keep anyone from hearing.

Before I left, I checked the windows to make sure they were tightly closed. A little water came in under one of them, and I folded a towel on the wooden sill to catch it. The view of the river was good from here; it stretched wide, rushed angrily, brownish in the gray light of early morning. I could see what looked like half a house, tumbling, and then a wagon. At the place where the river had cut across this little peninsula, there was a lot of debris piled up, caught against a large, uprooted tree.

I could see no sign that the water had fallen at all. It still lapped halfway up the front lawn. From the back window I could not see to the Kentucky shore because of the rain, but I had a good view down into the courtyard. Past the buildings I could see what looked like a boathouse and a dock which still seemed to be intact. A boat could land there. Red or somebody might come back if the storm continued. I wished I could think of some way to signal.

When I opened the door to start down, I could smell coffee, bacon. I could hear the radio. On the second floor I paused, my hand on the knob, ready for instant disappearance if that kitchen door at the bottom of the stairs should open.

The news was in progress, and I wanted to hear it. "Worst flood since . . . disaster area declared in . . . crop and property damages into the . . . seven lives. . . ." And then, "Skies are not expected to clear until late tomorrow night or early Sunday."

I almost wished I hadn't heard that forecast. I was leaning against the sticking door carefully, hoping to open it without noise, when the radio was turned off and a man's voice said, "Clearing late tomorrow. Or maybe Sunday. God damn it, those fools don't know any more than we do."

Mrs. Kinsolving's voice said smoothly, "It will clear, son. It always has. How many eggs?"

"Two. Christ, every morning you ask me. Two eggs like I'll be having all summer, it looks like."

"You act as if it were my fault that you can't get out of here, Kenny."

123

"I'll tell you what's your fault, Maw—"

"Don't call me Maw."

"I'll tell you what's your fault, Maxine. That smart-ass idea you had for having that girl stay to dinner."

She said, "I explained the whole thing to you. What else could I have done?"

"You could have killed her, Maw."

"Stop calling me Maw!" Her voice was sharp. I heard the sizzle of eggs being slid into hot fat, and then she went on more placidly: "I think it would be a mistake to do anything to the girl. Up to now we've been very careful."

"I've been careful. I come by the river, go by the river. Nobody ever sees me. You're the one people see."

"*I* have been careful, son. I go to a different store each time. It has been quite a lot of trouble, but I think it's worth it. I can handle my part of it, and I can handle this girl, too. She's too dumb to be much of a problem. And I have made sure that when she leaves this place, she is never going to want to think back on anything that has happened."

"This is too sweet a setup to take chances."

"There's less of a chance my way. Oh, by the way, I've been meaning to ask you something. That night. I sent Kathleen down here and told her to ask you to help dig a hole."

"What?"

"I told Kathleen to ask you to help her dig. She doesn't have any strength in her arms."

"She didn't say anything to me. Not that I can understand half she says."

"You don't try. You have never had any patience with her. Here are your eggs. And then when you've finished

124

breakfast, I think you'd better go out there behind the barn where I told her to dig the hole and check."

"Check?" There was a snort of laughter. "Use your head, Maxine. If she didn't bury it, by now the rats have checked."

Chapter 10

I PUSHED against the door, so weak and sick I could hardly open it. Back in my room my teeth were chattering with a nervous chill as I drew the blanket up over me. I knew that I had been pushing myself beyond the limits of my strength. After having a baby, one should rest, take things easy for a while. I was a product of centuries of pampered women—all those Cabbots with two *b*'s. I should have known I couldn't just pick up the hoe.

But I had to. The danger that I had only sensed before was real now. I didn't know how I could ever cope with anybody as coldly calculating as Kenny Kinsolving. Why, I wondered, was this such a "sweet setup"? For what reason did Kenny come and go by the river? And what did Mrs. Kinsolving buy when she went to those stores, a different store each time?

Maybe she wasn't buying . . . maybe she was selling something. The silver? What if she used the bent kitchenware only because the silver drawers were empty? Old silver had quite a bit of value, and so did old china— maybe she would start on that next. Those portraits in the lower hall were too recent, too postcard-pretty to have much value, probably, but the ones in the upper hall had a crudity that might class them as American primitives; she could get a good price for them if the craze for them was as big around here as it was in New England. Or maybe there were rare books. Just recently I had read about a first edition of one of Poe's books selling for many thousands of dollars. I got excited, sure I was on the right track.

My chill was forgotten now, and my mind felt sharp. Today I was going to do something constructive. First, I would examine those guns in the rack. I got out of bed and found that I could reach them easily by kneeling on the desk. Nervously, I held them away from me, scarcely knowing how to find out if they were loaded. The thought of myself trying to shoot anybody or even threatening anybody with a gun was almost ridiculous, but I didn't know what all I might have to do to get out of this house.

But the guns were empty. I should have known that a boy with military school training wouldn't leave loaded guns around.

Up there in the tower room this morning I had wished I could think of some way to signal. I knew nothing about the Morse code, never having been a camp fire girl or a girl scout, but I remembered seeing a Boy Scout handbook among the books. I found it, turned to the index, and looked up signaling.

"It is fun," the book said, "to send a message from hill-top to hilltop or across a lake. . . . Signaling at night with flashlight is easy."

It sounded easy. Tonight I would try it. I didn't try to memorize anything except the very simple SOS signal— three short flashes, three long flashes, three short flashes. The beam of the flashlight was weak, and through the rain there might not be much chance of catching anyone's attention, but I felt it was worth a try.

I was standing by the window as I read the book, and

that bird out there was watching me with bright eyes. Her wings had more spread to them now, as if they sheltered fledglings. The bright-breasted male came with a worm, and when the female moved from the nest, I saw four ugly, naked heads rise with great, open beaks. He rammed it home down one of them, and I wondered how he could keep track of whose turn it was.

Those birds cheered me, they were my good-luck omen. If they could make it through this storm, so could I.

Kathleen came with my breakfast tray around seven thirty. Some white roses, rain-battered, were bunched tightly in a jar. I said, "Thank you, Kathleen—I love white roses." She bobbed her head. Kathleen seemed jittery this morning, but then she always seemed jittery.

I got back into bed and made myself eat, although I wasn't very hungry. There were two eggs for me, too. The bacon was cold, probably left over from Kenny's breakfast. The coffee tasted warmed over, too strong, but I drank it, knowing I needed it.

Mrs. Kinsolving came into the room and stood looking down at me. I still had on the dark silk robe. She said, as I had known she would say, "What happened to the white bathrobe?"

"I put it somewhere—" My voice was vague. I leaned to look around on the floor as if I thought I might see it. "Maybe I left it in the bathroom. Or Kathleen might have picked it up and put it in the laundry. It was stained."

"Indeed. I hope you realize that we are in no position right now to run a laundry service. For instance, there will be no clean sheets for you this morning."

I said I didn't mind. And then I looked up into the big, cold face and said some of the words I had figured out to say: "Mrs. Kinsolving, there is just one thing I want from this house—" I tried to make my voice fit her conception of me. "I would just love to have one picture of Matthew when he was a little boy. That's the only thing I ever want you to give me. Antiques, old dishes—they bore me. My own home is just full of that old stuff. But if I could have just one picture of Matthew—"

She said grudgingly that there might be one around if she could find time to look. Surely I must realize that she had many things to do.

I put jam on a piece of toast and added, trying to make it sound convincing, "All I want is just one picture. No matter what you might want to give me when I leave, I couldn't take anything. Lying here with nothing to do, I've decided that I'm going to Australia. One of my best friends lives in Australia, and she's just dying to have me come. I've got just about enough money in the bank for a one-way ticket. I probably won't ever come back."

I looked up into the pale eyes, wondering if I had been too obvious. "My daddy will have a fit when I go to Australia." I looked down . . . my "daddy" would have a fit if I ever called him anything but Father. "I bet he's having a fit right now—he was expecting me home days ago. I've just got to send him a wire or call him as soon as I can. How long do you think it will be before—"

She said shortly, "Who knows? The rain is supposed to stop by Sunday. Sometimes the water goes down quickly. Sometimes it takes a week or more."

"A week?" I wailed. "Oh, no. But . . . well . . . if anybody should come out there in a boat like that man did the other day—" I put on a dumb, wide-eyed expression. "Poor Daddy, I know him. I wouldn't be one bit surprised if he hasn't already got the FBI out looking for me. Daddy and I are so close."

"Finish your breakfast."

I pushed the bacon aside and finished the last bit of

toast, knowing I had been far from clever. Surely a child could have seen through my words. *All I want is a picture; the rest is yours. I am going to leave and never look back.*

And those idiotic words about my father and the FBI. I only hoped her investigation of me hadn't gone far enough to find out that my "daddy" hadn't written me once since the letter he had sent me when Merriam College expelled me.

She walked over to the window. "Take the tray, Kathleen." And then I saw that from her pocket she was taking a hypodermic syringe and a small vial.

Kathleen leaned to take the tray. I grabbed hold of her hands and said loudly, looking up into her face, "I must not . . . be put to sleep anymore." But there was no help for me in that poor face.

Mrs. Kinsolving was coming toward the bed with the needle ready. "Lie back. Roll up your sleeve quickly, and let's not have any nonsense."

"No." I folded my arms tightly. "I don't want to be put to sleep anymore."

"Don't be foolish. You need your rest."

"But I do rest. That's all I do. Please, Mrs. Kinsolving —" I wasn't faking anything now.

She reached for the alcohol. For one crazy moment I thought I would throw myself on her mercy and tell her about the baby. But I knew I'd be a fool to count on any mercy from her. I knew I'd better not let her know there was any thought in my feeble mind but leaving this place and never coming back.

Her strong hands were on me. In spite of all I could do, she was drawing up my sleeve. Over her shoulder she spoke to Kathleen: "Help me. Hold her like this." The moonstone eyes moved close. "If you get one of these needles broken off in your arm, girl, you'll wish you'd been more cooperative!"

I gave a sob and lay back. The alcohol was cool on my arm. The needle was close. Kathleen was holding my hands the way her mother had told her to. And then she let them fall, stepped back. And I knocked that hypodermic clear across the room.

With a ringing slap Mrs. Kinsolving struck Kathleen across the face. The girl stood there motionless, the marks of her mother's fingers slowly reddening. Mrs. Kinsolving picked up the hypodermic syringe and looked at the bent needle and then at me.

"Damn you." She said it calmly. "I have another needle, of course. Plenty of needles, and I can play games as long as you can. Bring the tray, Kathleen."

They left the room. I thought she would come back with another needle. But I would strike that one from her hand, too. And the next, and the next . . . Oh, God, help me! I cannot let myself be put to sleep again today!

A few minutes later I heard Mrs. Kinsolving coming up the stairs stiffly. I got out of bed. I felt strong. I would fight her. She stopped in the doorway, looking in at me with venom in her eyes. But the ivory head was at a regal angle, and there was almost a smile on her face. She drew the door toward her, closed it. I heard a key turn in the lock. And then the key was withdrawn.

I rushed to the door and grabbed the knob. I cried, "Mrs. Kinsolving—please don't lock me in!" I hammered on the door with my fists.

The footsteps receded.

I went berserk. Like a crazy person, I walked up and down that room. I had to get upstairs to that baby!

The window . . . that little balcony. The window was

131

hard to open, swollen with rain. I pressed my face against the wet screen, but there was so much ivy that I could not see how close that next window was. I could climb out onto the little balcony, I thought, maybe get down to the next window and into the next room. I tried to open the screen, but it had been painted in.

With one of the guns from the rack I battered at the screen until it came loose. But when I leaned out into the rain, I saw that the little balcony stopped short of the next window by a good four feet. I caught hold of one of the thick wrists of ivy, tugged, and found that it held tight to the stones of the house. I tried to think. If I could make Kathleen understand what I wanted, she could go into the next room, open the window, reach out her hands from that balcony. . . .

Sweat popped out all over me. Dear God, I must be insane! Kathleen had very little strength, and I had less right now. I closed the screen, the window. I got a towel and wiped the rain off my hair, my face. It frightened the wits out of me to think that I could even have considered such a harebrained plan. If I fell, my baby up there would die. Never in my life had anyone depended on me before. It shocked sense into me. I felt important as I had never felt until now.

In the drawer I found dry pajamas; I could not even risk catching a cold. While I was putting them on, another idea occurred to me. There had been no key in the lock on that first night. Perhaps I could find a key in one of the drawers.

Golf balls; tees; a Mickey Mouse watch; a tie clasp in the shape of a polo mallet; studs; a Boy Scout badge; a life-saving patch; some loose foreign coins. The history of Matthew's boyhood was in those drawers, but there was no key. The two small drawers at the top of the chest had been searched thoroughly; now I felt around under the clothing in the others.

Under the paper in the bottom drawer there was a lump. I lifted the paper and saw something wrapped in tissue. It had not found its way there by accident; it had been hidden. And from the look of the yellowed tissue, many years ago.

The pearl. I carried it to the window. Lumpy, bumpy, as Matthew had said last summer. Flushed with iridescence the way the river had been on that last night of fair weather. *Matthew, Matthew. . . .* I turned the pearl in my fingers. It must have been some job for the poor oyster or whatever to make a pearl this size. I said between my teeth, *Matthew, I am not just lying here with a rock in my eye.*

It was a sign, a very good omen, I told myself as I wrapped the pearl in its tissue again and tucked it into the coin purse in my straw bag. I was going to get out of this room; I didn't know how just yet. I was going to get out of this house with Maria safely. There would be a way. Someday, I would have that pearl attached to a chain to wear around my neck as a good-luck charm. I thought positively, visualizing that pearl on a thin, gold chain.

I went on searching for the key. Standing on a chair, I felt along the dusty top of the door facing, thinking that a tall person like Matthew might have put it there—though for what reason I couldn't imagine. On my hands and knees I felt all along the edges of the rug, knowing the key might have fallen, bounced. I even managed to move the big chest.

No key. I stood in the middle of the room, tired but not ready to give up. There would be some way; there had to be.

Kathleen was coming. It was time for my bath—another

of those little nurse types of services that Mrs. Kinsolving seemed conditioned to. If Kathleen were alone. . . .

But when the door was unlocked, Mrs. Kinsolving stood there too, plainly irritated that because of me she had to climb these stairs so much.

She cleared the bedside table and placed a thick towel on it before the pan of water was set down. When I started to get into bed, I pretended to grab for support and knocked the pan of water to the floor. Kathleen fell to her knees and started mopping with the towel. Mrs. K said an unladylike word and went for more towels. As I had hoped she would.

I grabbed hold of Kathleen's shoulders. "You must find me a key—get all the keys you can find and bring them up here and try to unlock this door the first chance you have. I have to get upstairs to feed that baby. Do you understand me?"

She gave me a blank, scared look, but there was no time to say any more. Mrs. Kinsolving was coming back.

She threw some old towels on the floor. "No bath for you today," she said. She picked up the empty pan, took Kathleen by the arm, and left, locking the door.

A bath was the least of my worries. I only prayed that Kathleen had understood.

It seemed that I had a long time to wonder. I tried to pick the lock with a nail file. I straightened a bobby pin and tried using that. I was starting to try to take out the screws that held the lock mechanism in place when I heard Kathleen coming.

I knelt there, agonizing, while she tried one key and then another. She kept crooning to me in her own soft language.

The lock turned. The door opened.

I hugged her close and then took her face into my hands.

"Listen. Put all the keys back where you found them. Don't forget." I gathered up all the scattered keys that lay on the floor, put them into her hands. "Do you understand? Don't let anybody see you doing it."

She bobbed her head as if she understood.

I locked the door and slipped the key into my pocket and hurried to the other end of the passage. Nobody was in sight below when I peered over the stairs. I crossed the hall with the leaning ancestors. At the door to the back stairs I had a bad moment. The door had swollen even more. Perhaps I had closed it too tightly before. I had to tug on it hard, making a frightful noise when it opened.

Again I hesitated, fearful that I had been heard and that the kitchen door down there might open. But Mrs. Kinsolving was talking in that loud, hollow voice of hers, telling Kenny about the spilled water. "I swear, I think she spilled it on purpose."

There was a cry from above. Kenny said, "Listen . . . I keep thinking I hear that goddamned cat. Like it's shut up someplace and can't get out—"

But I was halfway up the stairs. I caught up my child and hushed her next cry against my breast.

Chapter 11

It worked all day, unlocking the door and then locking it again. Maybe some of my luck just had to be good.

But there were some narrow escapes.

I had recalled that Allegra used to talk about self-demand feeding. Under the circumstances it seemed sensible not to let Maria get hungry enough to make any demands, so I tried to get up there to her about every three hours.

Along about the middle of the afternoon I had the key in my hand and was about ready to unlock the door to go upstairs when I heard footsteps that sounded like Mrs. Kinsolving's. She had already been up over the stairs twice today; I knew she wouldn't be coming unless she had a good reason.

Maybe Kathleen hadn't put the keys back, so that now Mrs. K suspected I had one. I looked around the room for a place to hide the key quickly, knowing that she would look first in my pockets and then in every other place in the room where a key might logically be hidden. I slipped it into the hem of the draperies, an easy, but not too obvious place.

The door was unlocked while I was still by the window. She said, "The cat seems to be shut up somewhere, crying. Is she in here?"

"No. She doesn't like me very well."

"Have you heard her crying?"

"No." My mouth was dry. "Maybe—maybe she's outside somewhere."

"In this rain? Hardly." She looked around the room, muttered something about maybe she'd better go downstairs and get her hearing aid, and then left, locking the door behind her.

Did this mean that the baby had started to cry and that Kenny had heard her? Had he even now—God, please!—started looking around the house for the cat?

"Kitty, Kitty—" Mrs. Kinsolving was calling out in the hall.

With fumbling fingers I took the key from the drapery hem and hurried to unlock the door carefully and peer into the hall. She had not gone downstairs but had started opening the other doors on this floor.

There was a thin sound above the noise of wind and rain. It sounded like Maria. A gust of wind shook the house, drowning the sound, and then I heard it again. It was Maria. The doors kept opening.

If Mrs. Kinsolving went up to the third floor, she might be able to hear the baby without her hearing aid. Or if Kenny came up. . . .

From here I could see the door to the back stairs, and I kept my eye on it. I didn't know what I would do if I saw her pull that door open and start up. Run after her? And then what would happen?

"Kitty—where are you?"

A fawn-and-brown shadow came running from the direction of the main stairway. The cat, the beautiful, beautiful cat. I sagged against the door, half sick with relief. I heard Mrs. Kinsolving speak sweetly in that voice people use to cats: "There you are, you naughty girl. Where were you hiding, pretty thing? Why were you crying? Come, I will feed you."

I barely waited for her to get downstairs before I locked my door and ran across the hall. The sticking door. The sound of the radio, loud, in the kitchen, but up above there was that lusty screaming, steady now. No cat in the world ever sounded like that. Not even a Siamese.

In the tower room I snatched up my daughter, quieted her furious demands. And then I sat on the cot and rocked back and forth with her in my arms. How long could this go on? How many more frights like this would I be able to survive?

That night around eight thirty I was thinking it was nearly time to go upstairs when Kathleen came and tapped on my door. She had something to tell me, but I couldn't make it out. It seemed to have to do with Kenny or the keys, perhaps both. Her eyes rolled, and she was as upset as I had ever seen her.

I was upset, too, but I knew I could listen to those pitiful sounds all night and never understand a word she was trying to say. I patted her shoulder. "It's all right, Kathleen. Don't worry. I am going up to the baby now."

"Bay-ay?"

She said it eagerly. I knew she wanted to go up with me and see the baby, but I was afraid to let her. "You had better go back downstairs now before they miss you. Here, let me swap flashlights with you—yours has a brighter light."

She handed over her flashlight. She would have done anything I asked her to do.

We left the room together, and I locked the door. We moved along the dark hall with her just ahead of me. She always made a noise, even though the hall was carpeted. I was just opposite the linen closet and about to step out behind her into the big hall when she froze.

In a loud voice she said, "Keh-hee—"

The door of the linen closet was ajar, and I slipped into it. Through the crack of the door I got my first look at Kenny Kinsolving. He was almost at the top of the main staircase. Kathleen's flashlight was on his heavy face, showing me the ruddy cheeks, a tawny forelock, curly, over light brown eyes.

"What the hell are you doing up there?" His voice was an angry whisper.

There was a stammering of frightened sounds.

"Oh, for God's sake, Kathleen. Shut up, and come on down these stairs."

Her feet hurried unevenly as she went past him, and then I heard the stealthy brush of other feet. Kenny was coming on up.

I flattened myself against the shelves of the linen closet and pulled the door as nearly shut as I could. He made little more noise than the cat as he walked past me along the narrow corridor. I barely heard the sound of the doorknob as he tried my door. I wondered if his mother had sent him up to do a room check. Thank God I had locked the door. He went back down the stairs.

For a minute I stood in that linen closet, my breathing loud in my ears as I waited for more footsteps on the stairs. Had Kenny, in spite of Kathleen's flashlight beam in his eyes, glimpsed me in the shadows behind her or heard a sound that made him suspicious? Had he gone down now to tell his mother that she must come upstairs, unlock my door, and see for herself whether or not I was in there?

I knew I would have time to get back into my room if I heard her start up the stairs. The house seemed to move a little, sigh a little as I waited in that stifling closet, but nobody came.

The tower room. My baby's sweet, frantic mouth at my breast. When she was taken care of, I went to the window with Kathleen's bright-beamed flashlight. Through the rain I could see a few dim lights over at Always and the moving headlights of a couple of cars.

I began the slow signaling: three short flashes, count three; three long, count three; three short. Over and over I signaled just the way the book had said to do. There must be somebody over there—someone who had been in the service, even a boy scout—who would know the Morse code.

A boat went by on the river once, and I thought I had been seen. The big searchlight circled, sweeping the dark water, and the boat went on. I knew my chances of being seen by anybody out on the river on a night like this were pretty slim. They would be scanning the surface of the water, not looking up.

I tried not to think about what would happen if Kenny, for any reason, should go outdoors and see my flashing light. I tried not to think about the possibility of another room check.

Somebody was signaling: A light over there went on, off, on, in a rapid succession of dots and dashes that would have been unreadable even if I had taken time to memorize the code. I began a frantic, stepped-up signaling.

And then I stopped. It was only a leaf, nothing more, trembling between me and one of the lights over there. The brief flare of hope exhausted me. When I finally got down to the big firm bed in Matthew's room, I set the alarm for Maria's next feeding, slipped it under my pillow, and fell instantly asleep.

But I dreamed uneasy dreams of flashing lights and

phone bells ringing. I woke, thinking my alarm had gone off. But I had only been dreaming. The luminous dial showed me that I had slept one hour.

Saturday. The continuing rain and the constant fear were beginning to get to me. I started worrying for fear I wouldn't be able to hold out much longer, not only physically but mentally. Those people out in the hall were beginning to seem real. I couldn't rid myself of the notion that their painted eyes followed me. That they listened with me, holding their breath. That they whispered about me, worrying.

Saturday afternoon I opened the trunk in the tower room. There were old clothes, books, and a big box of letters. I thought that the letters might fill in some of the gaps in my knowledge, but to my disappointment they had all been sent to Maria Kinsolving at the time of her husband's death. One had the seal of the governor of the state on it; one was in pencil on ruled paper. Most of them said about the same words of sympathy over and over, and only two had lines that were of much interest to me.

One said, "Does your young Matthew still bring in every bird with a broken wing? I know what a comfort he must be to you. . . ." And another said, "You have a kind heart, Maria, but do not think of taking your sister-in-law into your home to live with you now that you are both widowed. I know Maxine has had much misfortune, particularly with poor Kathleen, but she has never been your friend. She is envious. And she is much too indulgent with Kenny. . . ."

On Saturday night I heard the phone ringing. I was upstairs with the baby, and this time I knew it was not a dream. It was fairly early in the evening, and I had been about to go downstairs for a couple of hours to wait in my room in case there should be a room check before bedtime.

I stood on the stairs, listening, and could hear it plainly as it rang several times down in the kitchen. Kenny answered, said a few words I could not catch, and hung up.

My mind was jumping. So there was a working phone in this house! For some reason or other it was not listed under Kinsolving in the phone book, and for some reason or other Maxine had lied about it.

My mind took another jump. *What if that phone in the sewing room had been dead because it was a portable phone, not plugged in?*

I could call somebody for help! But whom could I call? Red? I didn't even know his name.

The police? I knew that in an emergency like this they would be working around the clock. What could I say? That I was frightened? That I thought my life might be in danger? Many people must be frightened, must know that their lives were in more certain danger.

Miss Gee. I hadn't given her my name, but I knew she would remember me. She was capable; she would know what I should do. She had authority, too; if she called the police, they would listen to her. I didn't know her first name, nor where she lived, but with a name like Gee, even in a big city like Cincinnati. . . .

I waited several minutes and then stole down the stairs. There was no sound now from the kitchen. Once inside the sewing room I shut the door carefully. My flashlight showed me the phone over there by the sewing machine. I went over to it, praying.

The cord was trailing. I put the beam along the baseboard and saw a jack connection. I plugged it in and got an instant dial tone. My fingers were shaking as I dialed *O*. There was a wait and then a voice said, "Operator."

142

In a low voice I said, "I want to call a Miss Gee in Cincinnati. I don't know the first name or the address—"

"The initial G is all you know?"

"No, no. The name is Gee—spelled *G-e-e*."

"One moment, please. . . ."

While I was waiting, I heard a click, a sound on the line as if another phone had been picked up. Instantly I pressed the button so that the person who had picked up the other phone would not know the line was in use.

I hurried back to my room and locked the door. It wasn't two minutes after that I heard my doorknob turn cautiously.

"Who is it?" I tried to sound sleepy.

There was no answer. Steps moved back along the corridor, uneven, as if they lurched a little. Kenny. If those uneven steps meant he had been drinking, I hoped he would be drunk enough so that he would have to go to bed and sleep it off.

I would wait awhile before risking another call. But when I got back to that phone again, I would call the police as I knew now I should have done before.

But when I got into the sewing room later, I saw that the phone had been removed.

I thought back, remembering that my finger had been quick on that button. Kenny couldn't have known for sure that I was using that phone. But evidently he was taking no chances. And now he had good reason to suspect that I had found a way to get out of my room.

I thought of trying to get downstairs to use that other phone. Maybe later I would get up my courage, but it seemed to me now the risk was too great.

Upstairs in the tower room I had a kind of desperate feeling that this had to be our last night in this house. I signaled, nursed my child, signaled again until my finger on the flashlight button got sore. I changed hands. *Somebody, anybody*. The rain had lessened now, and the few lights over there were brighter. It didn't seem to be asking too much for one pair of eyes to look over here, notice that there was a flashing light coming from this tower.

And then, please, whoever you are, tell somebody. Even in the morning, tell somebody!

I slept for a while with my head on the windowsill. There was less wind, and the house was quieter around two o'clock when I started downstairs. My sandals were so loose now that it was an effort to keep them on my feet. I didn't dare go barefoot because I knew it would be a dead giveaway if the bottoms of my feet were black in the morning.

There was silence down in the kitchen. Kenny, long before now, must have gone to bed. I stood there, weighing the risk. It wouldn't take me two minutes to get to that phone down there and call the police. What I had to say could be said in about ten words. I started down.

Two eyes, bright and evil on the stairs coming up from the kitchen. It was a rat, motionless in the circle of light. I all but screamed, all but fell as I scrambled back up the stairs making all kinds of noise.

I closed the door of the tower room tight and with my flashlight went all around looking for a hole, a crack that might be big enough to allow a rat to squeeze through. There wasn't even space enough for the smallest mouse, but I had heard horror tales of rats and babies, and I was taking no chances. I slept there on the narrow cot with the baby the rest of that night.

Toward morning something woke me. I lay there, alert and apprehensive, listening to the difference. It was beginning to be light, but there was a different quality to the light.

The rain had stopped.

I got up and hugged my robe around me. All around us was that water, still rushing, but it would go down now. I looked toward the place where the road would emerge eventually and saw that a lot of debris had lodged against the big, uprooted tree, making a sort of dam. I saw what looked like a chicken coop, a mattress. How many days before that driveway would be usable? Yesterday she had told me it might be a week or more.

But I wasn't going to have to wait for that road. A boat would come for us today. I took a deep breath, planning my day. When the sun came up, I could take a piece of the broken mirror that leaned against the wall and catch the rays of the sun and signal with that.

As I stood there, the clouds took on color. At first they'd had only an iridescence, like my pearl. Then quickly they were pebbled with lavender, rose-pink. In sudden splendor then the rim of the sun shot a blaze of glory across the face of the waters. I tried not to cry, but thankfulness welled, hurting. Today was the day!

I visualized somebody over there right now telling somebody else about the light in the tower last night. Listening, it seemed I could almost hear the words. I visualized that boat putting out from the shore. Here at this window I would stand watching. I would call down when the boat was beached. And then, with Maria in my arms, I would go out of this house. I saw myself stepping into a boat with Red—yes, he would be the one—putting out his hand to help me. I felt the strong clasp of his hand steadying mine. I felt the water move under the boat as we crossed safely to Always.

What positive thoughts I had that morning.

As I took care of the baby I remember that there was an odd little island of calm. I whispered to her, and it seemed

145

that she looked at me. She yawned, and I marveled at her skill. She opened her tiny hands, no bigger than spools of silk thread, and I told her fortune, knowing only my wishful thinking for her long and happy life. I talked baby talk and was a little amazed to know that I sounded exactly like Allegra.

Soon, soon, we would have real diapers, not just these towels. I saw those diapers, felt them against my hands, fluffy and soft, as I folded them the way somebody would teach me. We would have real baths, not any more of this messy business with mineral oil. I saw exactly how Maria would look in her first real bath, loving it. I smelled the delicate fragrance of that baby powder Allegra used.

Yes. Today a boat would come.

Chapter 12

THERE IS a good reason for my remembering—I think pretty accurately—the time at which each event took place: my daughter made me a slave to the clock. It was a little before seven when I closed the door securely that Sunday morning and went downstairs, one step at a time because of my flapping sandals. No rat lurked now on the second-floor landing. Maybe the cat caught it. I told myself that there had been only one rat in the house, and the cat caught it. In my mind's eye I fixed a firm picture of that fawn-and-brown cat catching that one gray rat. One rat; there were no more.

I could smell coffee, hear the radio down in the kitchen turned up loud, but I did not stop to listen. The rain had finally stopped, and that was enough for me. Every time I went back to my room there was always a moment when I held my breath, a dread that when I opened the door, I would see Mrs. Kinsolving sitting there waiting for me. But there was no sign that my absence had been discovered, although this time I had been out of my room for several hours.

Good. I locked the door again and slipped the key into its hiding place in the hem of the drapery. I opened the window and looked at the sky so beautifully blue with its promise of no more rain.

For a few seconds it alarmed me that the nest seemed to be empty, but then I saw the mother robin swoop low with something in her beak. The nest came to life with four clamoring little mouths.

Relieved, I went and lay on the bed and tried to make some more constructive plans.

It was good that the rain had stopped, but I knew now with the house so quiet that I would have to be extra careful about making a noise when I left this room. Above all else, I must keep the baby from crying. She had slept longer between the last couple of feedings; this could mean that she had made up that day or so she had missed without any food and from now on would be less demanding. If I could manage to get upstairs by nine thirty or even ten, we ought to be safe.

Mrs. K would be coming up before long to unlock the door for Kathleen to bring in my breakfast tray. She would make another trip shortly after when the door would have to be unlocked again for my bath. With luck, that would be her last trip upstairs until noon.

I hoped it would be possible for me to let Kathleen have a glimpse of the baby sometime this morning. It had worried me all along to think that she might try to go up there when I wasn't with her. I had worried about the possibility of her trying to light that kerosene lamp, for one thing. And now there was the extra necessity for keeping the door to the tower room shut tight on account of the rats.

Resolutely, I put those negative thoughts out of my mind. All would be well. Today that boat would come. Over there now, maybe at a breakfast table, somebody was

148

reporting having seen the light that flashed from the tower last night.

For a minute I wondered if it would be a good idea to hang a sheet or something white outside the tower window to flutter in the breeze. But I decided against it. Now that the rain had stopped, it was almost certain that Kenny would be going out into the yard to have a look around. He might shoot some more rats. I recalled his words about coming by the river and going by the river, and I wondered if he had a boat out in the boathouse I had seen in back. At any rate, he would be likely to go out to see if there had been any damage to the big dock.

A noise outside the window. It started with small sounds of scolding protest, then rose to shrill alarm.

I rushed to the window and saw the cat crouched on the limb of the tree just outside the window. Motionless, except for the twitching end of her dark tail, she was less than a dozen feet away from the robin's nest. She inched forward. The bright-breasted father bird swooped low, pecking at her and crying angrily, but she swiped at him with her paw and moved closer.

The mother robin just sat there, hovered over her babies, her eyes bright and frightened. The cat's belly was low on the limb as she moved a little closer.

I had to do something! I looked around the room. If I could poke at her, knock her off . . . my eyes lighted on the guns. I grabbed the longest one, opened the screen, lunged. But I couldn't reach the cat. She didn't seem aware of me when I yelled at her.

The robin dived again, lit on her back. She whirled. Feathers flew as she tried to catch him, but he got away. She moved closer to the nest. Crouched. Sprang.

Both birds were in the air now, circling the nest and screaming distractedly. Other birds took it up. Feathers drifted down; leaves and drops of moisture flew from the tree. I saw the Siamese seize the first little bird.

I slammed the window down and walked up and down the room, my clenched hands pressed to my mouth. It was not a bad omen . . . I would not let myself be such a fool as to believe that. It was only the balance of nature. Life. They were only birds. They would have other babies before the summer was over and never remember this first nest of little birds.

But my nerves were shattered now. I could not get back my good feeling about the day.

I thought: Why did that mother bird leave the nest? Why didn't she stay there, fight that cat, die if she had to die to save those babies?

The birds were still crying, still circling their empty, torn nest when my breakfast was brought upstairs. I looked up at Kathleen when she set the tray before me and saw that her gray eyes were darting in that uncontrolled way. I knew she wished she could tell me something.

Mrs. Kinsolving was coming into the room with fresh linen. She loosened the sheets at the foot of the bed with a jerk as if she might be about to rip them off with me sitting there eating. She told Kathleen to go downstairs and get the water for my bath, and then she said with a toss of her ivory head, "Give me the key."

I had just picked up my coffee cup. I stalled by taking a sip before I put it down. "What key are you talking about, Mrs. Kinsolving?"

"You have a key to this door. Don't bother lying to me, my girl. You have been coming and going as you pleased. You have been prowling this house."

"What on earth makes you think that?" I put on a face of blank innocence.

"Oh, I am not entirely deaf. I can hear certain sounds

and vibrations perfectly well, even without my hearing aid. Don't think you have been fooling me. Tell me at once what you have done with that key."

I pushed scrambled eggs around on my plate, took a bite, made myself swallow. She wasn't going to mention the phone—that would have involved an admission that she had lied to me earlier when she had said there was no phone. And anyway I had the feeling that if Kenny had been sure I was on that line, he would have done more than just try this door last night. Had they heard me in the early hours this morning when I had seen that rat? No; there would surely have been an investigation before now. Something else had clued them in.

I went on forcing myself to swallow food as she stood over me. Out of the corner of my eye I could see the way the big hands clasped and unclasped.

"The key is hidden somewhere in this room, of course. Don't think I can't find it."

My voice sounded calm: "If you think there is a key, go ahead and look for it."

She seized the bathrobe and thrust her hand into the pockets with such vigor it's a wonder she didn't tear them off. She felt then between the mattress and springs, jostling me so that my coffee sloshed over a little. She went through the drawers, moved books on the shelves, shook the contents of my straw bag onto the desk, turned back the edges of the rug.

I made myself go on eating.

Kathleen came back into the room. She carried the basin of water for my bath and placed it on the desk where the contents of my bag were strewn.

Mrs. Kinsolving towered over me, her color high and her breath coming fast. "I know you have a key, so don't bother me with lies. I know Kathleen found one for you.

Why else would all the keys be missing from the doors? If you do not tell me where that key is hidden, I shall give Kathleen the beating of her life."

I stared at her, unbelieving. I looked at Kathleen, who stood motionless, her wide, scared eyes moving back and forth from her mother to me.

I whispered, "No . . . don't. . . ."

"Where is the key?"

No words would come. I couldn't let them. A great sickness lurched inside me, grew.

From the inside of the closet door she snatched down a leather belt with a metal buckle.

I pushed my tray aside.

The strap whizzed through the air and cracked around the cowering girl's shoulders. I bolted from the bed and ran into the bathroom and threw up.

When my nausea had spent itself, I washed my face in some water saved from yesterday and brushed my teeth. I heard nothing more from the other room. My face in the mirror was pale. There were no brown spots on it now, but there were dark circles under my eyes.

Between my clenched teeth I said a prayer: *God . . . kill her.*

Back in my room that woman was stripping the bed as if nothing had happened. Kathleen stood there, her arms piled with crumpled sheets. There was an ugly welt on her bare arm.

I drew her into my arms, sheets and all. She was trembling. I kissed the welt and smoothed back the untidy dark hair from the poor face. I smiled at her through tears. "I love you, Kathleen. I love you."

She answered me in that strange, other-world language of hers and placed a kiss against my cheek. It was loose, moist, like the kiss of a very young child. I drew her close, and she leaned against me as if tired.

Mrs. Kinsolving hadn't missed anything. She turned for one hating look when she left. "I know you have a key." But now, I sensed, she was not quite so sure.

When she had gone, I wondered, exhausted, if we had scored a small gain. I put everything back into my bag—the coin purse, lipstick, the tissue-wrapped pearl that had gone unnoticed in her furious search. I bathed, and as I took the last clean pair of pajamas from the drawer, I told myself that this was the last pair I would need.

The good feeling of optimism I'd had early this morning was gone now, but a grim determination had taken its place. I knew that, physically, I would not be able to continue much longer with this fearful marking of the hours. This had to be the last day.

I rested, sitting at the desk until I felt a little better. The house which had sighed and wheezed constantly in the rain and wind was quiet now. It seemed to be waiting, listening. The sun, absent so long, showed everything clearly now, sharpening edges, brightening colors. I hoped my mind would sharpen, move out of the shadows of this past hour.

From the hem of the drapery I took the key. A thorough search of this room would find the hiding place, I knew, but I would take that when it came, if it had to come.

Without a sound I locked the door behind me. Without a sound I moved along the narrow hall to the larger one where I peered, as I always did, to make sure there was no one to see me. It seemed to me that the ancestors in their portraits leaned a little farther from the walls to help me look. The coast was clear.

Across the hall the sticking door opened much more easily than it ever had done before, as if the last person to come this way had not really shut it at all. On the other side of it I had a surprise that caught me up short. The sugar cartons that I had noticed in the sewing room were stacked here at the top of the stairs. Apparently somebody was about ready to take them down to the kitchen.

I sucked in my breath and stood unmoving, listening. Kenny might still be in the sewing room. But then down in the kitchen I heard him asking his mother what she had done with the rat poison. She told him to go look in the barn.

I started up the stairs, my mind occupied with the stacked boxes. What was in them—salable items from these upstairs rooms? A thought hit me, almost floored me. Cautiously, I moved back down for another look at those cartons. The printing said each carton held twenty-four, one-pound boxes of cube sugar.

I opened the carton on top. It still held cube sugar. Each of the boxes on the top layer had been opened. There was no doubt in my mind but that the others had been opened, too.

Dumbfounded, I went on up the stairs. It seemed to me that I could still hear my roommate Jeannie's voice again: *Two drops of LSD on a sugar cube. . . . Imagine, it costs me five dollars.*

Another voice, Mrs. Kinsolving's: *I have been careful. I go to a different store each time.*

She had been buying the sugar, not selling the silver, as I had suspected.

I could just see her, queenly, descending from her Lincoln, the very social-looking type who could so easily be imagined entertaining at tea after tea and murmuring,

One lump or two? I could imagine her in that sewing room, too, her ivory head bent over her clean, profitable work, as she dropped two drops of the mind-blowing drug on each cube.

It came back to me now, the gritty feeling of the cutting board. I had thought it was gritty with dust, but if I had tasted that dust that night there in the darkness when I groped for a pair of scissors, I would have tasted sugar.

Kenny's voice: *I come by the river, go by the river*. With the clearing of the weather he might have started moving his stock downstairs, preparatory to leaving. I had no idea how many cartons in that room contained sugar, nor how many cubes there were in each one-pound box, but the cartons had been labeled twenty-four pounds.

There was a fortune stacked on that second-floor landing alone.

The tower room was brilliant with sunlight. I had not seen my daughter in the bright sun before. She lay with her violet-blue eyes wide, as if she, too, sensed the difference in the day. Her skin was pink now. I could see the delicate veins in her forehead, the translucency of her incredibly small ears.

She yawned and said a word: "Ah-h."

I gathered her into my arms, this warm, lightly breathing miracle. Peace moved into me again. I was so happy as I fed her.

I remember that. Happy.

But I could not dawdle this morning; I had work to do. Covering my hand with one of the towels I used for diapers, I pried a shard of broken glass from the mirror and began trying to catch the fire of the sun to spell out my message for help.

I kept my head as low as possible so I wouldn't be visible to anyone who might be out in the yard below, but I could see clearly to the place on the opposite shore where the water came halfway up on the trees and on some of the houses. Several people had come to the water's edge. Something seemed to have attracted their attention, and it looked as if they were trying to pull it ashore.

Or . . . my pulse quickened . . . they might be trying to launch a boat! They might have seen my signals!

I stopped trying to spell out my SOS and concentrated on trying to shine the light right in somebody's eyes. *Oh, look up over there, somebody, anybody.*

But if they noticed, I saw no sign of it. I kept on trying, but I knew that with the sun so bright on the water there were millions of reflecting ripples. I could hardly expect that those men over there, so intent on something at the shoreline, would notice one more bright flash of light.

Discouraged, I rested after awhile, my arms on the wooden sill. In a minute I would have to start trying again. Over at Always I heard the chime of church bells. Sunday. I counted back the days until Thursday night when I had first started coming up here and could hardly believe they were so few. It seemed a lifetime.

Below, near the back of the house, Kathleen cried out. I went to the back window of the tower, standing so that I could see and not be seen. Kathleen was out at the little garden, and Kenny was advancing toward her from one of the buildings with his hand stretched toward her. Even from this height I could see that what he held in his hand was metallic, bright.

The keys.

She was carrying a basket which looked to be full of lettuce or some sort of greens. I saw her drop the basket and run clumsily toward the back terrace with Kenny taking swift strides after her. She was lost then to my view, but her scream rose to an unbearable vibrato. One chilling scream as she reached the terrace, that was all.

I stood paralyzed. I would stay here—they knew for sure now.

No, no. I must get back to my room, lock the door, prove I had not had a key.

My child slept. For a few seconds I hovered over her in an agony of indecision. But I knew she would be safer here. I closed the door and snatched off my loose sandals. Halfway down the flight from the third floor I heard Mrs. Kinsolving give a cry: "My God, what have you done to Kathleen?"

"She fell and hit her head. She's just faking. I'll carry her to her room."

"You hit her!"

"Yes, I hit her! I found the keys behind the barn—some of them—where she had thrown them. Go upstairs. This time make that bitch up there give you that goddamn key!"

I stumbled against one of the sugar boxes—there were more of them now—took time to straighten it. I pushed then at the sticking door, and it opened so suddenly I almost fell. I ran, making noise that even Mrs. Kinsolving could have heard if she hadn't been yelling at Kenny down in the hall.

It wasn't until I was in my room with the door locked that I realized I had lost a sandal. I didn't know for sure where I had lost it—maybe in the hall, maybe on the stairs —but I knew I didn't dare risk going back to look for it.

I put my head back against the door and thought: Is it over?

Many times since I had come to this house I had paced

up and down in this room, trying to think what I could do. I went now and sat quietly by the window. I could hear them moving around now in Kathleen's room just under mine.

I thought: Is it over for you, Kathleen?

I remembered the tired way she leaned against me this morning. The child's kiss. The bewilderment in the strange, broken eyes. I hoped she had understood me when I told her I loved her.

The robins were gone now. I looked at the torn nest and thought: I must plan.

But my mind was as empty as that nest.

I looked down at the wreck of my nails. Somebody was going to have to come out here and help us. I didn't know of anything else I could do.

The key to the door was still in my hand. *Kathleen*, I had said, *put back the keys*. That had been my most stupid move. I should have known she couldn't fit all those keys back into the proper locks, nor even understand why it was necessary to do so. It was easy to imagine her, in terror, throwing them out behind the barn.

Mrs. Kinsolving's footsteps were coming along the hall. I leaned and put the key into the hem of the drapery, not knowing why I bothered when my telltale sandal was sitting out there in the hall or on the back stairs. Or somewhere.

I heard her fitting her key into the lock. Did I dare ask her about Kathleen? I wondered if it would have been possible for me to have heard that scream if I had stayed in this room. But maybe that didn't matter anymore now.

The door was opening. Over my shoulder I said, "Is Kathleen all right? I thought—maybe I'm wrong—but I thought I heard her scream a little while ago."

"Oh, she'll be all right. The poor girl stumbled on the terrace—it is so wet and slippery—and had a nasty fall. But don't you worry. You have nothing at all now to worry about."

Something about her voice. . . .

I turned. She was smiling at me warmly. The Mother-of-the-Year was back.

Chapter 13

She said, "I have such good news for you, Francesca. A man is downstairs—"

"A man?"

"Yes. He came in a boat—"

"When?"

"Just now. Just this minute. He said he would be glad to take you over to the village. Now you can get in touch with your poor daddy so he won't have to worry about you anymore. Do hurry, child. You must get into your clothes right away."

I was on my feet. I pressed my hands hard against my trembling mouth, almost unable to believe it. But why should I question this good luck? I had known that today would be the day. I had known someone would come!

I started tearing at pajama fastenings. *My baby. I would go right up and get her. They couldn't hurt us now with that man down there.*

She got my tan dress from the closet, my underwear. "Is there anything of yours in the bathroom?"

"Yes . . . no . . . I don't know."

She left the room, and I fell into my clothes, fumbling with the fastenings, lapping over my underwear with safety pins. How emptily this tan dress hung on me, this tent that I had sworn once I'd never wear again. I noticed then that my missing sandal had been placed by the bed. I put it on, no more confused by its sudden reappearance than I was by any of the rest of this sudden switch.

But I thought I saw through her change in manner. Belatedly, she was realizing that she had gone too far with me and now was trying to make amends. Oh, but there was a day of reckoning coming for her and for Kenny, too. I could hardly contain myself at the thought. How lucky I was to be leaving this house before they had guessed how much I knew about them.

She came with a comb I had left in the bathroom.

I said, "Where is that man now—the man who will take me to the village?"

"He is waiting for you down in the kitchen."

I tore at my hair with the comb. "Is it the bus driver—the young man?"

"My goodness—" She laughed, her strong teeth shining. "I would hardly ask him what he does for a living, now would I? I am just so grateful to think that he would bother when there is so much trouble everywhere. There now, do you think you have everything?"

I looked around the room, not really caring. I picked up my bag, paused as a sudden thought struck me. "A boat, you said. But I didn't hear any boat—"

"No, of course not. It's a rowboat. It's tied up around at the back."

"Oh. But is it safe—a rowboat, with the river so swift and all that debris?" Uneasily I thought of how weak I was, the danger there might be for the baby.

"Oh, Francesca, you really are a little landlubber, aren't you? A rowboat is safer than anything!" She gave a jolly laugh and took hold of my arm. "It is no distance at all over to Always."

Don't get the baby now. In the hall I got that message so strong, as if the people in the portraits were whispering. *Wait until you get downstairs and know it is safe.*

I stood there and hesitated, resisting that hand on my arm as I listened. There was no sound from above. There was no sound from below. But that was to be expected. Kenny would hardly be down there chatting with the man who had come for me. He would be keeping out of sight.

"Come *on,* child."

I followed her down the stairs like the stupid, nothing girl she thought me to be.

"Right back here," she said. "He is waiting for us in the kitchen."

We went through the short, narrow hall that led to the kitchen. She opened the door and said, "Francesca, this is the man who has come to take you to Always."

A man sat at the table. He got up and came toward me. It was Kenny.

Chapter 14

As I sit here now writing down, crossing out, reaching back for the exact sequences and timing, I am very sure of one thing: My life was saved because my recognition of Kenny Kinsolving did not come in one stunning flash. I would have cried out. My face at least would have betrayed my horror.

But he was sitting at that kitchen table with a drink in his hand and his back to the door when I walked in. There was a second, maybe two, when I thought: *He looks like Kenny . . . that mane of tawny, wavy hair.*

He put down his glass and stood up and during those seconds I was thinking: *He is the same height, the same heavy build. What shall I do if—*

On one hand I saw a ring with the head of a lion and a diamond in its open mouth. He turned, and I saw the face I had seen in the circle of Kathleen's flashlight.

Fear swept over me as if the river itself had poured through the door. I stayed on my feet. I breathed in and out. I said something.

Behind me, Mrs. Kinsolving was saying some words: ". . . from the village . . . so fortunate . . . terribly kind. . . ."

Senselessly, I echoed her words, my mind grabbing this

way and that. Shall I scream? . . . run? . . . fall to my knees and beg? . . . lunge for one of those knives in that rack on the wall? . . . hope for some miracle that will let me get at that phone?

The woman's hand was on my elbow. "Come now. We must not keep him waiting any longer, Francesca. He has already been so patient. The boat is right out at the dock in back. Don't be afraid . . . perfectly safe. . . ."

Her hand was urging me forward lightly. Her strong, yellow teeth were bared in a smile of reassurance.

I thought of that Nazi Ilse and those others. On the way to the gas chambers they told the victims they were being taken to the showers. Easier that way, less strain on everyone concerned. Come quietly. No struggling. No pleading. No screaming except at the end.

The boat. A quick blow. The river accepting one more body. Mine.

We had moved now through the kitchen door into the bright, smiling day. I had the wild hope, based on nothing, that help might have come. I would break from them and run screaming toward that help. But no one had come. No one was going to come. Whatever was to be done, I would have to do.

Kenny had not spoken. I could smell liquor.

"Oh . . ." I stopped just outside the door. "I really must tell Kathleen good-bye."

"Kathleen is resting. She fell. Remember, I told you? I don't want her disturbed."

"But her feelings will be hurt." My teeth felt dry. "She has been so good to me."

"I know." The fingers on my arm tightened a little, and I had the feeling that mother and son exchanged glances over my head. "But we won't bother Kathleen just now. She doesn't understand anything anyhow."

We reached the terrace steps. "Oh . . ." I stopped, looked down, stirred through my bag.

"What is it?"

"Oh, dear. I forgot my pearl."

"Your what?"

"My pearl. Yes." In my idiot voice I said to Mrs. Kinsolving, "Imagine, I did find it after all! Matthew had hidden it in a drawer under some paper. It's that freshwater pearl he found. It's very large and really very valuable, I think."

"Where is it?" she asked.

"It's—oh, gee, let me think . . . I hid it again. I just can't think where . . . but I know I could find it."

Her moonstone eyes met the pale brown ones of her son. "Oh, I wouldn't bother now, do you think?"

Kenny said gruffly, "Let her get the pearl."

I went back through the kitchen alone. I glanced toward the phone. Could I grab it—dial Operator—hope to get a few frantic words said? No, no. It would be over for me then. I didn't pause on my way through the narrow hall into the big one.

Fear had me by the throat. *I must not run,* I told myself as I went up the wide staircase to the upper hall.

The ancestors leaned like corpses being tilted from their coffins. *Run.* They said it. *Run.*

At the top of the stairs I kicked off my sandals. I ran. I tugged at the sticking door, almost fell over the sugar cartons, ran up the bare stairs to the third floor.

Half falling, and with the strength almost gone from my legs, I made it to the tower room.

I closed the door and fell to the floor beside the cot, my breath coming in gasps. I put my cheek against Maria's, and she woke.

Had I, like the mother cat, only led them to this baby?

In a minute . . . two . . . five, at the most, they would come looking for me. And they would find me.

I got to my feet with the baby in my arms. *Help me, God.*

But there was no help.

At the window I looked across the wide, rushing river. *Send somebody.*

But nobody was coming.

The baby started to cry. *Please don't let her cry.* She cried again.

Mindless with panic, I walked up and down that room with her in my arms.

"Let me think!" I moaned the words out loud. "There must be something I can do . . . something!"

But there was nothing, nothing that I could do. I had no weapon. Even if I could get to those guns down in my room, they were useless—and they must know they were useless or they would not have left them there. Those knives I had seen in that rack in the kitchen would be useless even if I had them in my hands. The shards of glass in the mirror . . . I looked toward them hopelessly. How could I fight anybody when I had to hold this baby in my arms?

"Francesca . . . oh, Francesca. . . ." Mrs. Kinsolving's voice echoed sweetly through the house below.

I stood motionless, trying to hear where that voice was coming from. It sounded as if she might be calling from the big hall downstairs.

I licked my lips. I had . . . how long? Could I signal somehow in one last desperate attempt?

Yes. Yes. There might be a way I could send one last, desperate signal.

I put the baby on the floor on a pile of towels. I seized

166

the kerosene lamp and smashed it on the wall over the cot. I splashed some of the kerosene on a wooden beam and let the rest soak into the mattress. I opened the screen and, panting, shoved the narrow cot mattress halfway out the window. I lit one match and then another and jumped back as the flames caught. They were hardly visible in the brilliant sun.

But the smoke spiraled upward, making a dark signal against the sky.

I had destroyed our hiding place. We couldn't stay up here. I picked up my bag, and with the baby held tight in my kerosene-wet arms I left that room and started down from the tower.

Those other rooms that I had not been in on the third floor, the servants' quarters . . . should I hide in one of them as long as I could, hoping help would come in these next few minutes before it would be too late?

No. I didn't dare. I could hear the flames crackling up in the tower.

Mrs. Kinsolving was calling me again, angrily now. It sounded as if she might be back in my room.

Down there on the second floor I could hear doors being flung open. I told myself that if wardrobes and closets were being searched and beds looked under, I had a little time. By now, she would probably have Kenny helping her look for me. They would come up to this floor to look next.

There was a chance that if I hurried down now, I could make it to the kitchen and use that phone.

On the second-floor landing I listened beside those cartons of sugar. The smell of kerosene was strong on my clothes, on my bare arms.

"Francesca!" I could imagine the pale blaze of those eyes. Where was Kenny now? I looked down the flight of stairs that led to the closed door. Would I dare take the chance of going down there without knowing where he was?

There was a sound in the kitchen as if someone had stumbled over a chair. A growled obscenity. A popping noise as if a cork had been pulled from a bottle.

"Francesca!" The hollow sound of Mrs. Kinsolving's voice was closer as if she had come into the big hall just beyond this door.

I held the baby tight. *Don't cry,* I willed.

And then I heard Mrs. Kinsolving say, as if she might be leaning over the banister out there, "Kenny! I want you to come up here right this minute and help me find that miserable girl!"

I stood there, crushing the baby against my breast so she would not cry. My breathing was ragged. If Kenny obeyed his mother and went up the main staircase from the hall, I could get down these back stairs and try to use that phone. I would run then and hide in the barn. Or if they saw me, I would run down the driveway to the edge of the water. Somehow I would crawl out onto that big tree, screaming for help.

Eyes would have been drawn to that smoke and fire. Someone would hear me. Someone would see me. Kenny would not dare kill us in sight of that shore.

But what would I do if he should come up these stairs? He would be drunk by now.

My child was struggling in my arms. I crushed her closer and looked down to see that her face had turned lavender. I held her away from me. She gasped, cried weakly. And then she got a good breath and screamed her rage against all the world.

The door opened at the bottom of the stairs, and Kenny Kinsolving looked up.

168

It could not have been a very long moment, but it stretched. Glass in hand, his mouth slack, he stared upward as I stood there with my shrieking child.

Fear was a taste in my mouth.

He smiled at me and said softly that he would be goddamned. He put down his glass on the table behind him and reached for a bottle that lay on the floor. He started up the stairs then, looking at me from under his curly, light mane of hair. He had that bottle in his hand like a club.

I do not remember putting the baby down on the step behind me. I do remember picking up a carton of sugar and hurling it as he came up over those steps toward us. He tried to duck, but it hit him squarely in the chest. He staggered, dropped to his knees, dropped the bottle.

He groped, found the bottle, and started up those steps toward us again. His mouth was hanging open. His eyes were like the eyes of a tiger.

I threw the second box at his head. He fell backward, his mouth sagging open. I threw another box and another. He slid down headfirst, almost in slow motion, halfway into the kitchen. Lay there.

The little cubes of sugar were everywhere, on his face, on his open eyes.

I just stood there breathing hard, waiting for him to move.

He didn't move.

My baby was shrieking steadily, monotonously, on the stairstep behind me. I had barely enough strength left to lean and pick her up.

The sticking door opened. The woman's ivory hair was wild. She looked at the baby with her mouth gaping open. She said, "Why, you little fool—"

169

I said, "I think I've killed him. Kenny. . . ." I pointed down.

She looked and saw her son. She turned and seemed about to go to him. And then she gave one awful cry and lunged at me with her big hands all spread out and her fingers like talons. I fell backward against the stairs.

But there was somebody else here now, pulling her away from me. A man with hair that burned blessedly red.

Chapter 15

Miss Gee had large pearls in her ears. They were lumpy, bumpy, and they came from the river. She seemed to float above a great, shimmering desk. She said, "It is good to know yourself . . . know yourself . . . know yourself. . . ."

I struggled upward out of the river. "But I didn't know . . . I didn't know . . . didn't know. . . ."

A hand reached out. "There, now," said the hand. "There . . . there . . . there. . . ."

Jeannie stood at a window high in the sky. She said, "I can fly . . . fly . . . fly. . . ."

My baby in her pillowcase nightgown said, "Look, Mother. I can fly. . . ."

"No!" I cried out, clutching for the reaching hand. "Hold me. Hold me tight. . . ."

"I will," said Red.

I looked through my lashes. The dream was dissolving slowly. There was a bed, and I was in it, a circle of light, and I was in it. That hand was in the circle, holding mine. It was a strong hand with clean nails and hairs that were shining like fine copper wires in the circle of light.

Red's face was beyond the light, but I could see that

he smiled with that gleam of nice, even teeth that I remembered.

"There, now," he said. "There is nothing for you to be afraid of now."

My eyes drifted past him to the shadowed room to a window, a tall building out there with many squares of light. One of the lights went off, two. I thought sleepily, They are signaling. I slipped back into the dream. I had broken glass in my hand: no, a flashlight: no, a torch on fire. . . .

He was pressing my hand. "Don't you want to wake up and talk to me now?"

I sat up in terror, remembering.

He put his hands on my shoulders gently. "You're all right. Everything is all right. You're safe. You're in a hospital. Your little girl is doing beautifully—"

"I want her here—"

"She's in a nursery just down the hall. I think somebody said they put a bow in her hair. Pretty soon I expect they'll be bringing her in so you can see for yourself that she's all right."

I fell back against the pillows. "I . . . killed somebody. I killed Kenny Kinsolving." I covered my face with my hands and saw those dead-tiger eyes.

"He fell down the stairs." He said it carefully. "I think his neck was broken."

I opened my eyes and tried to free myself of that nightmarish recollection. There was so much that I needed to know. With difficulty I said, "Tell me . . . the parts I can't remember. Tell me . . . about Kathleen."

His hand patted mine. "Kathleen is all right. You don't have to worry about Kathleen."

I tried to read the dark brown eyes, but they were just

outside the circle of light. There were other eyes that I remembered, pale, like moonstones. "Mrs.—"

"Look, you don't have to worry about her, either. Just don't worry about anything."

"Did the house burn down?—"

"No, no. Nothing much burned but the tower. Everything was too damp."

A young nurse came swishing into the room and stood looking at him. "You'll have to leave now. The doctor would kill me." She batted her eyes at him a couple of times. "He said five minutes."

He got up. "One more thing. I talked to your father."

"My *father?*—"

"Yes. They found his name in your wallet on some identification thing. There's been kind of a big flap about all this, as you'll find out. Stories in the papers and all that. I thought your father might see something and worry. So I called him. He said he might drive out here."

I gave him what felt like a thin smile. "Did he also say that he might not?"

He made no answer to that, just leaned and tucked my hand under the sheet against the rough cotton of my hospital gown. "You just try to get a good night's sleep tonight, kid. Knit up the raveled. . . ."

"The raveled what?"

"Sleeve of care, honey. Shakespeare. . . ."

The pretty, young nurse watched him go. Then she turned her attention to me. She asked how I was, eased a thermometer into my mouth before I could answer, and then stood with my wrist under her fingers, looking down at her watch and smiling a little.

I took the thermometer out of my mouth to say, "Do you think he looks like Albert Finney?"

"A little. More like Peter O'Toole."

"Oh, never. Really?" And then I asked, "Do you happen to know what his name is?"

"Whose name?"

"His—that man who was just in here."

"His name? Are you kidding me? He told me that you two were— I mean, I thought. . . ." She stopped.

"You thought what?"

"Nothing." She smiled at me. "Just stop talking and put the thermometer back in your mouth, you lucky girl."

Chapter 16

HIS NAME, I found out, was Henry Fitzpatrick.

I had been trying out my name with boys' names ever since I was about six years old, and Francesca Fitzpatrick was too much, even if he had been my type. But I would never forget him, and I would send Christmas cards and, very likely, knowing my needs, someday send him a wedding announcement. I was only sorry I didn't like the name Henry well enough to name a child for him. Under the circumstances, it would have been a nice, grateful gesture.

On Wednesday of that week my daughter and I were released from the hospital. Maria by then weighed seven pounds and four ounces, which was very good, and I weighed only a hundred and three, which was very bad.

There was a rather upsetting bit of red tape before we left. They had to have proof that Maria had been born. I didn't see why they couldn't just look at her and make out a birth certificate, but the head nurse brought a young man to my room and said there was this form which had to be filled out within ten days of my child's birth according to Ohio law.

The young man sat beside my bed, his pen poised. "Who was the attending physician?"

"There wasn't one."

He gave me a look. "There was a midwife?"

"There was a . . . I don't know . . . there was a woman . . . I think she was a nurse. Yes. . . ."

"A woman. You think she was a nurse." He repeated my words soothingly, as if he thought I might be mental.

"Well, I know she was, only—"

"There is a space here for witnesses to sign. If you will just give me her name, I can probably get her to sign it before this has to be filed with the registrar of the district."

The panic had started. "I don't want her name on that." I didn't care if he did think I was mental. "I don't ever want to have—to have anything to . . ."

The nurse intervened. "Let it go. This girl has been through a lot. I think we can just have her sign, and then we can probably take care of the rest."

They put the form in front of me, and I signed it. The date? I didn't know that, either. They brought me a calendar, and I figured it out.

I was glad to be able to leave the hospital. We went to the motel on 52. My bags were still there, and it seemed sensible since it looked as if I was going to have to stay around here for a while. Everybody was very reassuring, but I was responsible for the death of Kenny Kinsolving, and there were certain legal formalities which would have to be observed.

Red—I won't try to call him anything else—drove us there in a Volkswagen, which was quite old and pretty crowded with the three of us and a large bunch of glads which Miss Gee had brought to the hospital. I had asked a nurse to call her, and she had come at once. I loved Miss Gee.

I wore—what else?—my tan tent. Although it had been

washed, I thought it still smelled of kerosene. The baby was wearing her only dress, which was one Red had gone out and bought for her. It was in sort of bad taste, too fancy—lace-curtain Irish, my father would have said. But then my father is a snob about people, and I am only a snob about clothes.

Red had told me the dress was a present for Maria, even though I had asked him to buy it. In the car I told him that I wanted to pay for it. "Oh, yes, I insist. I don't want to be under any obligation."

He took his eyes from the road to look at me, and I added, "Joke. Just for my life and Maria's." Primly then I said, "I am, of course, extremely grateful and always shall be. How much was the dress?"

He passed a truck and said, "Seven ninety-eight, plus tax. I nearly fell dead. And I will let you, since you insist, because I have one more payment on this VW and can't really spare that much money."

I mention all this because there were about three days after that when I wanted to occupy my mind only with things like seven dollars and ninety-eight cents, plus tax; and washing my hair and brushing my teeth with my own toothbrush; and bathing Maria in the big washbowl at the motel with a nice, soft towel laid in it.

I might also mention in passing that she hated it. She screamed, and I got the idea that she was hooked on mineral oil.

There was an afternoon when I spent about half an hour trying to put on eye makeup. I wore myself out and finally cried and washed it all off. On that same afternoon a woman came unexpectedly from one of the Cincinnati papers wanting to do a story about all that had happened.

She had this big camera with a flash thing you hold in your hand, and all she wanted was a picture of me and the baby, plus a few other little things about where I was born and where I went to school. Also, how did I feel about everything now, and would I do it all over again, and what were my plans for the future?

Her horn-rimmed eyes kept peering past me into the motel room, as if she were trying to get a look at the baby. I kept narrowing the door opening and murmuring, "No . . . I'm so sorry, but no . . . no. . . ."

She smiled widely and said she had a living to make and had come all the way out from the city just to see me. I really was sorry about everything, but I wasn't up to thinking about the papers yet. I hadn't seen any of them, but Red had already told me they had quite a few of the "facts" wrong.

That had been a relief. That had suited me better than if they'd had some of the facts right. I could imagine what some copy-hungry feature writer would make out of the story of my life.

A couple of days later Red brought a man from the district attorney's office to see me, but I'd had plenty of notice, and by then I was able to put on some eye makeup and a little lipstick without having my hand shake.

We sat in the motel room. It was close and stuffy in there, in spite of air conditioning, but at least it was private. I couldn't seem to get over my dread of having strangers looking at me.

The man from the DA's office was fairly young and extremely nice about everything. His questions were delicately phrased, and he didn't pry into anything that wasn't pertinent.

I told him some things that weren't really pertinent, I guess. About the rats, for instance, and the fact that I was terrified of the smallest mouse.

But it seemed when I talked about all that had gone on

in that dim, mushroom-smelling house, that I talked about somebody else. I felt as if I were recalling scenes from an old, worn-out movie film in black and white. Only the eyes in that house seemed to stand out sharp and clear . . . Mrs. Kinsolving's; Kathleen's; Kenny's. Even the rats' eyes. Even the watching eyes of those ancestors in the upstairs hall, although I knew he would think I was crazy if I told him about them.

He wrote down quite a bit of what I said, and then he looked from me to Red and shook his head. "There isn't any case for a homicidal charge. This girl had to do what she did. I am pretty sure the DA will agree. I doubt very much if this case will even be presented to the grand jury."

He closed his notebook and got up to go. I told him that I would stay right here as long as necessary. We shook hands, and he said I would hear from him again in a few days.

At the door he looked thoughtful. "Oh, one thing which has nothing to do with anything except personal curiosity. Those cartons of sugar, each of them, weighed twenty-four pounds. My wife can't even lift a clothes basket for six weeks after she has a baby. I have to do all the laundry."

After he had gone, Red said, "Do you feel up to hearing about how things were from where I sat?"

I said I did.

"Then I am going to find us a long, cool drink, and we are going to sit just outside the door."

I shook my head. "No."

"Yes, we are." His voice was firm. "One, for propriety's sweet sake. Two, I am beginning to have claustrophobia. And three, you need the sun. You look as if you have been living under a wet board for about two years."

"Thank you."

We sat with the door of my room slightly open so I could hear Maria if she cried. The lounge chairs were very comfortable. Red turned mine so that I faced away from possible curiosity, but I still had a view of clipped green lawns and cheery red geraniums in black-earth beds that looked as if they had just been edged this morning. I wanted no more of nature unrestrained for quite a while.

While he was getting the drinks, I put my head back and my feet up and arranged the slits at the sides of my green dress modestly. It happened to be the most becoming dress I owned. I had been astonished to see how well I looked in it, but I guess every girl thinks her figure is pretty smashing after she's had a baby.

Out at the pool some distance away some kids were yelling and laughing. I took a sip of the drink Red handed me and was glad he had insisted I come out here. He had on a short-sleeved, white turtleneck which was flattering with his dark red hair. I wondered why I had ever thought he looked like Albert Finney or why that pretty nurse had thought he looked like Peter O'Toole.

He sat down across from me. "I'll take it from the top. When I first saw you through the window waiting in that motel lobby, I couldn't see that you were pregnant. I thought you were a little kid about twelve years old, and I wondered how come your folks were letting you travel alone. You had your head back the way it is now, and you looked as if you might be lost."

That was how I felt. I moved my loose wedding band back and forth on my finger, remembering. "Tell me something. When you came back on the bus—you know, to the Red and White Café—did you wait for me?"

"Yes. I went into the café and asked if somebody had picked you up. Bobby Pickett, the boy in there, said you had asked about a taxi and then just started walking down the hill toward the river road. He said you hadn't come back. I waited for you as long as I could wait."

Bobby Pickett, my friend the swinger. It was odd, fitting in names now like Bobby Pickett and Henry Fitzpatrick.

I said, "I thought about you waiting. You know, wondered if you would."

"Did you? Well, that night when I took the bus back, I talked to my Uncle Leo. If my uncle had been on the bus that afternoon—remember, I told you how he is—everything would have been very different. He would have been able to straighten you out on some of the things you should have known. First of all, he would have been able to tell you what everybody in the town of Always knew, that the Mrs. Kinsolving who was living in that big house out there was not your mother-in-law."

"I was in that house a couple of days before I found that out."

"This Mrs. Kinsolving, Maxine, was from an old Kentucky family with no money. It may have seemed like a step up when she married one of the two Kinsolving boys, Kenneth, but she got the loser of the family. He never worked, just ran through the money his father had left him. He died about fifteen years ago, and in spite of the fact that she eventually became deaf as a post she supported herself and two children by nursing.

I interrupted. "I just thought of something. I should have realized that she wouldn't have been likely to become so expert in lipreading in such a short time. She told me her deafness came suddenly last summer during an illness."

"She wasn't the one who was ill last summer—it was the other Mrs. Kinsolving. Maybe you know that by now.

That's how Maxine happened to get into the house—she was a nurse, and nurses are scarce. Your mother-in-law died sometime in August, and Maxine just stayed on."

"I have wondered if she killed her."

"Nobody seems to think so, not even now. There was a coroner's certificate of death, all in good order. Maria Kinsolving had cancer. It was terminal by the time her sister-in-law moved into the house."

I sat up. "Why didn't Matthew's mother let him know? He thought the world of his mother—he was always telling me how much I would like her. He would have come right home—"

"I expect he would have. But I doubt if she wanted him to know. According to my uncle, Maria Kinsolving was a brave and wonderful woman. Her illness came on quickly, but she knew she was dying. In just a few weeks she wasted to a shadow, and it may be that she didn't want her son to be needlessly shocked by the sight of her. Perhaps she wanted him to remember her as she had been."

I said with such regret, "I wish I could have known her."

He took time out to light a cigarette. "At the time of Maria's death, Maxine told all the neighbors that she had taken care of notifying Matthew. I believe she told everyone he was already in Vietnam, but I'm not sure about that. I do know that when she gave out the news of Matthew's death, she never made any mention of his having a wife. Everyone just assumed that the property, in absence of a will or any other heirs, had gone to Maxine's two children, Kenny and Kathleen. Nobody was very happy about that. Kenny wasn't very popular around there . . . he had supposedly gotten one of the local girls in trouble. He had dropped out of sight, but it did seem as if Maxine had the right to live in that house with Kathleen."

"I sent two letters to Matthew's mother after she was dead. Not knowing, of course."

"And Maxine was getting the mail."

"Yes. I heard nothing. I guess you wonder why I would come when she ignored me so completely—"

"It's none of my business, but—"

"I wonder, too." I lifted my hands and let them fall. "I was pretty confused along about then. I couldn't understand why she hadn't written to me, but Matthew had always told me how wonderful his mother was, and it seemed to me there was maybe some explanation that I hadn't been able to figure. I had to make plans and. . . ." I let my voice trail off. I would never admit to him that I had thought of adoption.

"Let me ask you something else." He leaned forward. "Why did you stay?"

I told him a little about how it had been, although I didn't tell him all. "She wasn't too unkind at first. Anyhow, she insisted that I stay to dinner. That night her car wouldn't start. And in the morning, the river. . . ."

"Yes. The lower part of that town and the other one down the river road get slammed every time there's the least bit of a flood. I have never been able to figure out why people stay there, but they just shovel out the silt and move back in."

"I heard a little about the flooding on the radio that first day before the power went."

"It was bad the first two or three days. Two elderly sisters drowned when they were trying to get to high ground in their car. The flooding came pretty fast when the dam broke, and everybody along the river road was in danger. We got them out of their houses as fast as we could—rowboats and all the usual—and up into the church on the

183

hill, where cots were set up with food and blankets. But all the time I kept thinking about you. I kept thinking that there was something I ought to do."

"ESP?"

"I don't know. Maybe. I kept asking people if they had seen you walking to the Kinsolving house, but I couldn't find anybody who remembered having seen you except for a little boy who said he had seen a fat girl—"

"Me." I swirled the ice cubes in my glass, remembering how big I had felt as I walked along that road.

"I tried to call out there. I knew there were telephone lines, but there was no listing for Kinsolving. It's understandable that Kenny wouldn't want a listing. Later, after it didn't make any difference, I found out that the phone was listed in the name of Stoddard, Maxine's maiden name."

I was glad to have that bit cleared up.

He gave me that attractive grin. "You were none of my business—I'm as bad as Uncle Leo—but that Wednesday afternoon I took time out to find a guy with a motorboat who was willing to take me out to that house. The distance wasn't so much, but by then the house was on an island in the middle of a river that was on as big a rampage as I could remember."

"I heard you knock on the door, call for Mrs. Kinsolving. She didn't hear. I had started having the baby by then. I got off the bed and tried to get to the window. I saw you—" I shook my head and looked out across the green lawns to the bright reality of red geraniums, the sharp, clean shadows of afternoon. I took a last, big swallow of the tart, cold drink.

"I believed her, of course, when she said she had driven you back to the motel. So I got busy up at the church. The usual. A kid came in with a broken collarbone, and I taped him up. We gave shots. I kept thinking about you, but I let Thursday, Friday, Saturday—all those days go by without ever thinking of the one, simple thing I could have, should have done."

"What was that?"

"I'll get to it in a minute. I'm trying to keep things in sequence. On Sunday—midmorning, I think—the body of a man was pulled from the river. He had been in the water about four days."

My eyes widened. "Sunday morning. I think I saw that. I was looking out the tower window, and I saw some people down there at the edge of the water. I couldn't tell what they were doing—"

"They have found out since who the man was—somebody from the next little town—but they thought then it might be Kenny Kinsolving."

"Why?"

"Well, the build and coloring were about the same. Kenny hadn't been seen around there for quite a while. Not since that girl's father went gunning for him. Nobody knew he even came home anymore. But when they got this man's description on the teletype, things started happening very fast. It moved right out of local hands."

I kept my eyes on his face.

"It seems that a heavyset man with light hair and light brown eyes tallied with the description of the person who was suspected of supplying drugs to all the colleges in all the towns on the river—not just the Ohio, but the Mississippi, too, all the way from Pittsburgh to New Orleans. LSD. The one called speed, which is methedrine and very big right now. Some that aren't even illegal yet. You name it, and Kenny supplied it."

185

"But I don't see how you happened to come over to that house when you did—"

"You will. Now, the Federal agents recently had concerned themselves also with someone who had quite a different appearance in this part of Ohio. A recent check had been made of grocery stores—maybe hundreds, I don't know—and some three or four clerks remembered having sold cube sugar to a tall, distinguished woman with white hair."

"Mother-of-the-Year type."

"Something like that. And one of the clerks remembered having seen this woman drive off in a black Lincoln. A black Lincoln is not a very hard car to trace in our part of the country. If it hadn't been for the flood, it's very likely the net would have closed before then."

I said, "Meanwhile, back at the river—"

"Just a minute. I didn't know all this then. All I knew was what everybody else knew, that a man had been pulled from the river, and maybe he was Kenny Kinsolving. The sheriff was there. He had talked on the phone to the state police and then to one of the federal drug men. There seemed to be no special rush about anything."

I closed my eyes again. The jittery feeling was back, the scrambled horror of that morning.

"Are you all right?"

"Yes."

"Let me fix your drink."

"No, thanks. But I don't think I'll be able to stand it if you don't get to the place where you—"

"All right. This is it. I went to the café to get some coffee. I don't think too many people could have showed up in church that morning—the café was half full—and that kid, Bobby Pickett, was all importance. He said he had

186

been out shooting rats in the middle of the night, and he saw a light. He said it looked to him like somebody was trying to signal from the tower of the Kinsolving place."

"I had a flashlight."

· "That's what he said it looked like. There were only about half a dozen people paying any attention to him— the rest were listening to the radio—and you could tell that even those who heard him considered the source. You know how he is, the kind of kid nobody pays much attention to. But I did."

"At last."

"Yes, at last I'm getting to the point. And I thought, Good God, what if . . . and I picked up the phone and called the motel. That was the one, simple thing that I mentioned that I should have done days before. They told me your bags were still right here. They had not seen anything of you since that Tuesday afternoon. But they had begun to wonder—belatedly—if maybe they ought to get in touch with the police."

I got up and went into the motel room to see if Maria still slept. It seemed as if I just had to walk around a little.

Red said, "Look. I know you're tired. Would you rather wait until later to hear the rest of this? I know I'm going into a lot of detail, but there's not a whole lot more to tell, and I'll cut it short."

"Good." I sat down on the edge of my chair. It was bothering me a whole lot more than I had thought it would.

"I'll hurry. The sheriff was up at the Always Garage, where the man's body was taken. I told him that I thought there was somebody over at the Kinsolving house who needed help. He said he would do something about it later, but right then he was waiting for the state police. This was about the biggest thing that had ever happened in Always, and he wasn't going to risk blowing it."

"I see his point.'

"So did I, but I knew something was wrong over there. I went back to the edge of the water. It was then that I saw the smoke. So I stole the sheriff's boat. I knew it was the fastest way to get the whole gang moving in to help."

I took a deep breath. "Red, I don't remember much except seeing you loom up in that doorway just as Mrs. Kinsolving came at me. I mean, after that it's kind of blank—"

"No wonder. You went into shock."

"She would—I guess—have killed us both."

"It's quite possible. She was hysterical when I dragged her away from you. She knew that her son was dead. And then she collapsed. And they took her to the same hospital where they took you and the baby."

I shuddered. "I'm glad I didn't know it."

He looked thoughtful. "I'll tell you something else that you may find hard to believe. At that time there was not a whole lot against her, no case really."

"How come? She was the one who had bought that sugar. I am sure she was the one who doped it in that sewing room upstairs."

"Sure, sure. And they found LSD, pure, in its crystalline form up there in that room. They found marijuana down in the kitchen and all those other drugs. But there was probably nothing they could hang on her, nothing that a smart lawyer couldn't get her out of. Those two had been making enough money out of all their dealing to have hired themselves the best half-dozen lawyers in the United States. You can figure it out—speed alone sells for about five times its weight in gold."

"Red, she'll hire a lawyer, and she'll get me for what I did to Kenny—" The terror was back.

"No." He shook his head. "She didn't know all that—

188

she thought the game was over. She knew that Kenny was dead, and she had adored him. That night in the hospital she broke a glass and slashed her wrists. She was dead when they found her."

I looked away. All those kids out there, happy, normal. The pool, a fake, safe blue, smelling of chlorine, civilized. . . .

He got up. "So that's enough for today. I think I've told you too much."

"Tell me something else. She told me so many lies that I may never get everything straightened out. I guess I'll just keep remembering questions. But did your Uncle Leo ever tell you about the—the taint in the family? There were several members of the family, she said, who were abnormal. Do you know whether or not any of that was true?"

"Absolutely true. But the taint, as you call it, was not in the Kinsolving family. It was in her family. According to my uncle it was one of those bred-out families where there had been a lot of intermarriage. He said there had been some cousins who were not normal, and I think he said an uncle."

I drew a long, thankful breath. And then I braced myself again. "Don't go yet. I want you to tell me about Kathleen. I have been asking you about her every time I've seen you, and you have always said she's all right. But I know— I just sense—that you haven't told me all there is to tell."

He sat down again. "The girl was severely retarded— you know that. From the time she was very young she was in one of those institutions that you read about—cold, dirty, cruel. It was closed by the state finally, and Mrs. Kinsolving had to take her last summer."

I shook my head. "Poor Kathleen."

His voice deepened. "I really haven't been lying to you

about Kathleen. Do you remember when you first asked me about her at the hospital, I told you that you didn't have to worry about her anymore? She *is* all right." His warm hand covered my cold one. "She died that same afternoon of a skull fracture."

I cried. He came and knelt beside me and put his arms around me. I clung, leaned against him for a few moments, knowing my need to lean and cling.

After a while he said, "There, now." He smoothed back my hair and looked into my eyes. "Are you going to be all right now?"

"Yes, I'm going to be all right." I turned from his searching brown eyes, aware of what tears must have done to my eye makeup.

He stood up. "By the way, you might like to know that your father called me again."

I looked at him, surprised.

"I thought he sounded like a pretty nice guy."

"Yes. Well, I guess he is. He thinks I'm pretty much of a lost cause. Did he tell you that?"

"Not in so many words."

I stood. I gave him a big, bright smile and then was suddenly too tired to hold it. I went over to the door. "Red, someday I intend to thank you properly."

"I intend for you to." He made a fist and touched his knuckles just barely to my jaw. "There's plenty of time. Meanwhile, try not to worry anymore about anything. Get rested up." He opened the door for me. "Remember, all's well that ends. . . ."

Nothing ever ends, of course. Everything that happens to you becomes part of what you are. But the fear blurs, the sadness loses sharpness, and some of the sweetness lingers like a song half remembered.

Sometimes I dream of Kathleen. I hear those strange, babbled sounds, almost like singing, in that unknown language.

I think of Matthew, whom I knew for such a little while and whom I will always remember with such love.

It is too soon to let myself think about Red.